THE MUTTERINGS OF A LAUREL

Laurel Arnell-Cullen

FABER **𝆑𝆑** MUSIC

Contents

PART 1

SPRING/SUMMER & THE RAINY SEASONS

'Effe, is it raining?'

I am confused by my feelings. Thinking about it, starting a journal is probably a bad idea as I cannot guarantee that I am the only person who will read it. Right now I am sat with a coffee at my favourite café: 'The Barge House'. Yesterday was great, but today not so, and I have spent most of my day watching television on the sofa, and organising my cupboards. I find being creative and productive alike lasts only in short bursts of days, and maybe I have exhausted myself of energy. So that's why I am now drinking the strongest coffee on the canal and waiting for it to rain.

Today is the type of day on which you may think of beginning many things, but you never seem to start, let alone finish. Like a book: that's what my thoughts are set on currently. They are pulling out the canopy now, on the side of the café, and the waitress is saying 'Effe, is it raining?', to which the other replies, 'No, but it looks like it might', and since I wrote that down three more 'it might rain's have been said.

The sky feels much like my head today: heavy, large, and around it people are waiting for consequence. Sometimes I wish it would rain, just to get it all over with. I don't think people would mind, but sometimes when my mind rains it doesn't dry up for a little while, and in postponing the downpour I may in fact be extending it, but I'm just not ready to get wet yet.

Monday, 19th June

Dark thoughts in the hot sun

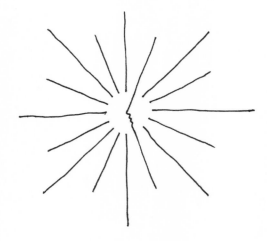

I am sat on a deck chair by the water next to my house. I am feeling hot like a red Marlborough being thrown to the road, after being stuck between your fingers. I see the man with no hair from upstairs watching me, watching the world, fuming off the floor in fluorescent smoke rings, pulsing through the daytime air, then he flashes his eyelids back to the sky. I think he is embarrassed for being caught peaking and must be able to see that I am turning furry, and that I am furious, and that my eyes are set so deep in their sockets that he might have mistaken me for a sleeping grizzly bear. But oh, I am awake, and even more so to your tendency to make me roar.

I am watching the baby ducks floating on the water, and the colour of my bare legs turning from a sickly pale to a healthy and quite attractive tan. Every sixty seconds my phone is projecting, 'We are sorry to keep you waiting, you are currently number five in the queue'. This is not why I have turned grizzly. It is because the who to whom I chose to give my whole self doesn't want to give it me back. He wants to suck on my thighs like a greedy mosquito. Although my father says: 'we shouldn't give to receive' I must say I think the ones who make all the rules might want to think about this a little more, especially when it comes to the realms of love and adoration. I suppose that they must have always been the ones being adored and not the other way around.

So whilst my feet were tearing up the paving slabs on my way home from the park, I got to thinking about the extremely loathsome way in which you buzz about me when I am trying to sleep, so that I wake up with an itch I never seem to finish scratching, so that my legs are red and sore and stained with valentine bites, so that nobody wants to ask my name when I drink wine in public places. I wonder if they think that sorrow on the skin is contagious. I suppose I have that juicy sort of blood which makes you want to feast, and I suppose you must be forever fighting a hunger at the bottom of your belly, for you to want to eat so very much of me, every day, before it turns into the morning. I move towards the house and when my feet stop being so ferocious to the floor, my hands take over and slam the front door, so that my terracotta sun descends from the very top of my window pane to the unkind concrete below. Even the sun is broken and ruptured today. I let out a humungous grizzly-wizzly-roar, and in that moment of sure silence you always get straight after madness, I realise the reason I am so enraged is because I am enraged with not you, but myself, and that really is a different sort.

I sit and wonder why I cannot make you love me better, when really I am meaning: why can I not make me love myself better? It is of these dark thoughts I sit and think in the hot, hot sun on a Monday afternoon, that make me feel as if I were drowning at the side of the water.

Beside a Benjamin

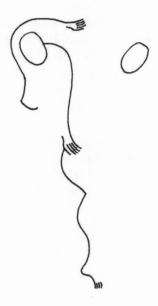

Last night upon returning home I stood on a slug. I felt him squish up through the gap between my big toe and the slightly smaller one next door, and without warrant we both let out a shriek, from what must have been each of our opposing realms of hell, whilst you were sleeping in bed. If only I had put my slippers on.

We woke up entangled and quickly separated our limbs, and then again in the night I aroused to my hand falling on his skin, shaken with a strange feeling – how is it stranger to touch now than not? In the morning, after a not so peaceful night for us both, we exchanged cold goodbyes, in such a way that it made me think soon after – is there anything about me that you ever loved? Just like that our love turns to hate, and time spent watching the ducks alone on the water in the same spot as yesterday seems much more precious, and every hour in my own company instead of his is a little more peaceful. When I find myself spooning heartbreak and eggs on toast into my mouth in the late afternoon, I don't really mind. Whilst sitting on the edge of the bank today I don't need a boat, but rather a pair of wings I can fly with. It is in my resolution of hatred for you that I can finally start loving myself again.

Saturday, 24th June

The shock of inevitable change

It's raining in Hoxton. I'm standing under the door
frame of Fortress Studios wondering whether to brave
the weather, which seems to be turning people into
drowned versions of themselves, or to stay hovering,
like a Casper, in hope that it may dry off. I have
been working in the studio, all weekend, on a sudden
whim that I really ought to mix this album myself. I
suppose there must be something inside of me which
wants all my hours of life to be occupied by only me,
alone, in lonely spaces. I wonder why that is. All
things considered, I cannot tell whether this building
is strange, or if my hours apart from the others have
made me stranger. You see, I only ever see the tail
end of a human here – legs and feet flitting around a

corner, the movement of the air from a ghost having just turned out of the bathroom before me. Today the studio door sprung open whilst I was making love songs in the other room, so perhaps these air movements are indeed ghouls.

I am walking now, on the pavement, toward the Vietnamese strip on Kingsland Road, in case you were wondering of my rainy movements. Olive is home from Paris today; I am beginning to wonder how I lived without her before we met. I hope we will drink wine together and she can remind me of how to shake my new unwelcome seriousness. These days I have forgotten what it feels like to be light. Instead I feel the weight of one thousand problems tied on a string from my belly button, pulling my top half down to meet my toes so that sitting up straight is a bit difficult and, although I'm not disabled entirely, making any quick movements is rather a waste of one's energy. Henceforth my decisions will become delayed, and although I will know what I ought to do, me and my one thousand problems will be inside a bubble which we will be afraid to burst, so instead we'll stay frozen in the most comfortable position we can find in that moment of fear, and stand hoping the fairy liquid will melt away, instead of pop, to avoid the shock of inevitable change.

Monday, 26th June

Uncontrollable urges

Yesterday, floating down the Regent's Canal sat upon a yellow inflatable dinghy, it struck me that this might be the best day of my life. Aperol Spritz in hand, oar in the other, and an uncontrollable urge to giggle, me and Olive might just be the best kinds of people that I know. We're also getting rather good at water sports. So last night I went to sleep with a wavy feeling about life, and whilst I was dreaming I must have found my rose-tinted spectacles, in my bed sheets, for when I awoke the world looked a little more sane and sunly, and full of things that are pink. Today my coffees have turned to rosé. It is 3.37pm, and I'm sat in a garden full of dusty blossom on the edge of Victoria Park, enjoying the weather and the wrinkles coming out of smiling eyes that pass. Fifteen minutes prior to this, I was cycling down the pathway, rehearsing a small speech for the imaginary woman I might find my imaginary lover in bed with one day, but I put that down to my tyres being flat making me a little on the raging side.

Tuesday, 27th June

Spring cleaning

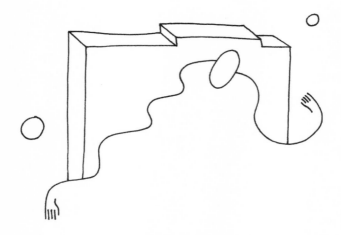

Hello Tuesday, I didn't sleep so well. Rain pours down outside my door, and I can only finish half my cup of coffee. All this time living alone has made me wonder: perhaps without your possessions to clutter my shelves, and t-shirts to fill my washing machine, I may feel only half of myself. So in attempt to make it feel all ok again I have been spending my morning-minutes cleaning up all different kinds of things. As I shovel the hot beans off the floor and into my rubbish bin, I wonder if we are always looking for something to clean or make more shiny. I shuffle my books along the bookcase and paint my staircase salmon pink. I tell you off for holding on a bit too long and w. you speak too loud in public places.

Are we all spring cleaning, all of the time?

Did you spring clean me, right out of your brain, because I was trying to get the dirt out from under your fingernails too often?

Or was it because I started to look curvy-wurvy then when the sun came out, next to all of your newer friends? Were you fed up of polishing my edges too?

The rain has stopped plopping on the floor now, and I'm sure somewhere outside there must be a rainbow. I will go now and walk in the puddles the sky has left for me. Perhaps along the way I can find an ice cold ice lolly, to match the temperature of my tumultuous thinker, in hoping that I can stay frozen just a while longer, perhaps all throughout the summertime. I suppose I may melt somewhere, with someone new again, and I suppose they might smell like fresh laundry and bleach from the toilet bowl. I wonder as I walk down the same familiar streets, will I still be spotting things to sweep away or might I wonder why I wasn't always this free and accustomed to berry stains on brand new white t-shirts?

I'm standing in the cold June wind, and above me the sky is falling. Around me people talk but no one is smiling, so I guess I'm not the only one. I haven't eaten yet and my belly feels swishy, full on one glass of Pinot Grigio; I like how this feels, but only when I'm feeling empty does my hollowness make me whole. Each bit of lard burnt from my body in butterflies leaves me a hungry skeleton, knobbling and wobbling, all over the concrete streets in the city.

I am an open book, my Mother Goose says. I wonder if everybody is a type of book. If so, I would like to be one of those pink leather diaries – the ones that have a padlock and a key, so that others think about what I might be thinking about, and so they invite me around for tea, and we will have discussions about all the things we have been collecting on our freshly pressed pages, whilst we've been locked up. I am afraid today I feel I am much more of an encyclopaedia, without the facts. No one rents me from the library because I'm far too heavy to carry home and much too long to read over the weekend.

When I am sad, I am most profound; perhaps that's why I spend minutes making teardrops for myself behind my eyeballs, to always remind me to write about the rainy weathers and the watery things. Upon my second wine swishing alongside anxious thoughts behind my belly button, I realise my pen and its short tip is most irritating, much like the man next to me chewing gum, and any moment I might realise I am much more like a very complex poetry book that, although is not locked, is most extensive in expressing itself in such complex ways, that only few might understand its use of pathetic fallacy in scenes of discomfort or delight. So although anyone can pick me up off the shelf and sift through my dusty pages, the ones who read me all the way through will be the only ones I'd ever want to read me anyway.

King and Queen

BERTON

The sky is large with jealousy this morning. As I look up I realise I have positioned myself perfectly between the gaps in the canopies, ready to get rained on. It's hard to write as I stabbed my thumb with Berton whilst I was giving him a haircut. I'm thinking how most beautiful things often come with sharp edges. There is only me and a caramel-skinned man, sat outside the deli. We are five tables apart, on opposing ends, as if we were king and queen at the heads of the table, spilling croissant flakes in the dining hall. Every few seconds he looks in my eyes and I feel awkward.

Wednesday, 19th July

Alone but not lonely

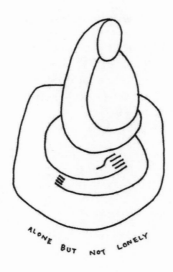

ALONE BUT NOT LONELY

It's 10am, and I'm making my heart race. I wish I had a monkey so we could have breakfast together in the mornings, when I'm alone. I look at the sky; he is looming above like a fat load of cappuccino foam. He's always foamy when I write. I am trying to think of what I'm thinking, but it seems my think-bubble is still sleeping on the mezzanine and has not yet joined me, even in the late afternoon. So instead of thinking, I've been staring at the seagulls, and the cyclists, and the cappuccino clouds. I chomp on my cheesy toast and wonder where I've gone. It would appear to me that Laurel left before I woke up, like a lover does sometimes at the first sight of sun in the morning.

I wonder how long it will be before she returns?

As I stare and my heart races ahead of me, I wonder where I will be next year. Will I stare some more at the sun from my orange bubble chair, letting the wind catch bits of me and take them with him? Will I be alone but not lonely?

Wednesday, 26th July

Cellotape

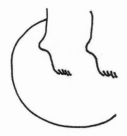

I lost my soul and my patience at Secret Garden Party. I thought I wasn't writing so much because I didn't need to escape so often, but escape I did. Legs running into the distance, mind left in a mud bucket, searching for salvation in a cup of flat cider. Swaying left, swaying right, and then onto the floor. I found that I quite like losing myself, even if sometimes I need a little encouragement. My only regret is that I didn't lose a little bit more.

Now that I am back, I am back to staring. Back to staring at the wind creating ripples on the water. Back to staring at the people in canoes, making their way through tides. Back to staring at the ducks, the tangerine and clementine litter, the leaves the trees fell out with, and all the other things that float past my house in the noon.

I lose myself for minutes staring at the things which float, and wish that I could too. Sometimes when you're heavy-hearted you weigh much more than you used to. I wish I too was disturbing the patterns on the water, instead of feet firmly on the earth, feeling more than grounded and rather still and stuck, as if I were cellotaped, so that when I try to move I cannot, yet when I look down at my feet all I can see are my shoes.

Thursday, 27th July

The collar and bell

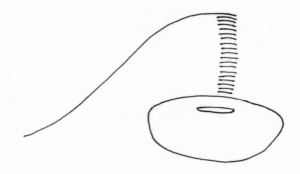

I have an hour to spare before rehearsals, so I am sat at my table outside whilst the rain makes spots on my notebook. A bright green vegetable truck has pulled up in the car park, and Ila the pussycat has gone to inspect, whilst the still-to-be-identified black panther is hiding under a chair, ready to catch her in flow. I do wish they could get along, but the panther is having none of it, and I have come to be thinking maybe she is jealous of Ila's collar and bell.

My mind is busy today and, much like just then, when my head was in clouds with pussycats, I'm distracted for ten minutes at a time thinking of pointless things and their pointless resolutions. I woke up in the worst sort of temper that only a god could calm down, but see, I don't know any so the whole morning I was a dinghy amidst a scorching storm, trying to navigate the raging seas. With little luck, my mother tried to dampen my fury but was instead faced with the snapping of crocodile teeth and five bin liners full with old clothes to take back to the motherland. After this I regretfully headed south of the river to Brixton, a place which will always remind me of kissing an ex-lover for a week too long. My meeting concluded in more plans, for making plans and plans again that feels all too familiar if you ask me, and usually results in my eyes glazed, thinking of other glazed varieties, such as doughnuts.

Saturday, 29th July

Hows, whys and whos

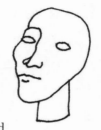

I wake up every day with the not-so-fleeting feeling of disagreement. I have a fury inside me that wants to blow brains and tell you how little I think of you. Between shouting and tears, I feel somewhere in-between my emotions that are unstable, unforgiving and unguarded. All of the un's. I want to fly far away, without any means of communication, to test my fear and see if it really means what it says. I don't want to talk, I WANT TO SCREAM. IN SHORT SENTENCES. I want to burst out of my body and into something new. I want to burst out of a giant pink frosted birthday cake, just like in the movies.

I am angry. I am just so angry. I want to stab with a knife. I want to jump from a tower. I want to cut so I bleed. I want to kick concrete bollards and eat beef phở until it comes out of my nostrils, and yet I cannot seem to articulate the hows, and whys, and whos. I feel my knees knocking whilst I test the temperature of my coffee with my tongue, sat on the side of the road. Knobbly bones vibrating all of that spite between my belly and my belly button, where I keep my most private emotions. I feel an ocean brewing in my tear ducts and a beating on my tongue. They should lock me away, before I do anymore harm.

Here and not there

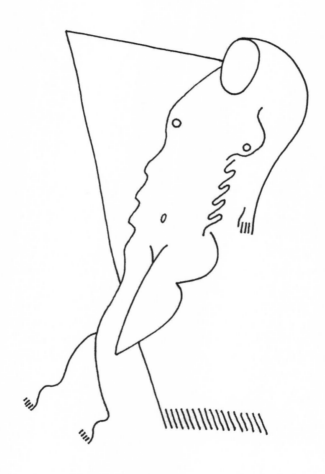

I'm sat in the park – the original PARK – it is Sunday and I am raining. I have my legs sprawled out on the spiky green, all over the east side, whilst I'm shielding my eyes from the sun, whom seems to have chosen only me to shine on in the park. My lids flutter like baby butterflies; they feel painful when they close. They said they haven't had enough sleep. I pull them tight, and fall backwards to the earth and wonder how to please them. As I'm laying, my dress tries to fly away without me; it has gone waltzing with the wind, who is making loud noises with the trees now, as if he wants all of the people in the park to pay attention to him. I landed back in England today, after a weekend of missing planes and trains and getting told off for being much too loud, much too late at night, in much too fancy places for a 'who' like me, and now that I'm back I'm back to thinking, which I seem to usually do when I am here and not there. I am unsure of these emotions that I feel, we have not met before. So you see, I don't know where to put them or how to package them up. They are flowing out of my mouth, like a red river flooding the town with blood. I flap my arms at my sides and blow the orange whistle, but nobody comes and I see bubbles streaming towards the sky as I drop towards the riverbed.

I stare upwards and, once the bubbles clear, I spot a little grey raincloud floating over the bridge. I suppose that he is lost from his fellow heavy friends, and I think of myself, as I often do, when I am only on my own. I think it might be nice to be a cloud and if I were I might look a little like him, floating all on my own with bits of grey. I wonder if he sees me see him as, before my eyes, his puffy shoulders cave and his hips melt until he is a bit like the shape of the slugs that slug across the laminate floors of my kitchen in the late autumn. His changing makes me feel all wrong and fat. As he slugs off down the sky-line I wonder ... did he grow into the type of cloud that reigns over the Hudson River? Suppose he did grow into that type of cloud, I bet he looked at his reflection in the canal water, in transition, and wondered who he was between, unsure of where he was meant to be or be going.

Smells better than it tastes

I'm having an Aperol on the side of Victoria Park. I can smell the scent of sugary nuts that they sell on the bridges, closer into town – that smell that smells better than it tastes, like gel pens, and cocoa butter shower gel. There is a group of people running around in circles, floating their arms up and down at their sides, as if they were human butterflies out at sports day, sweating in the summer. I catch my gaze from wandering and draw my attention back to my journal. This is the last clean page, and also the last still attached to the binder. So my journal has become more of a folder and so wherever I go I leave pages of intimate mutterings for someone to find and read, and judge me on my darkest speculations. I suppose they are more likely to throw my mutterings in the rubbish bin, but I'd like think life a little more romantic in the palms of a stranger.

A man with pure white hair and silver skin has been staring at me from the other side of the concrete pub garden. I think he is drawing me. I wonder what I look like in his eyes. I wonder if he would recognise himself on my page.

I wish that I was the type of person who would go over and say hello – not only hello but something quite intelligent in relation to our somewhat relation right now, and maybe we could both talk of why we are both drinking alone, whilst expressing ourselves on paper, instead of to people. He has gone now and, as sometimes it may be, actions following thoughts come too late. Instead the man with black eyes from behind the bar is walking my way. I put my head back in my folder and before I can see him, I hear Roux coasting past me on a skateboard, as if he were falling down the tracks of a rollercoaster, to save me from another solo drink and awkward avoiding of eye contact with the curious barman.

No time for tea

Reuben wants me to go for tea with him. I do not have the words to tell him that his words are not enough for me anymore, so instead I give him no words. I'm sure he will soon know just what that means.

Getting rainy indoors

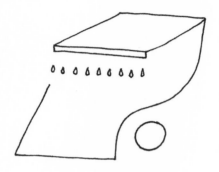

A large rain cloud has appeared on top of my house. I feel like he might fall very quickly. We do not have much time. I am peering out of my doors and into the windows of the people that live across the river. I try to see if the rain cloud is hanging over them too, but I'm not sure he is. I can see the sun reflecting off their windows and it makes me feel hot, so I take off my scratchy jumper. I feel the first spits on my cheek bones, and wonder how I'm getting rainy when I'm standing indoors. The noise of the kettle behind me is loud – so much so that I do not notice until he stops bubbling: the sound of my breath taking in, and puffing out, quicker, and harder than usual. I let out a sigh and the storm begins. I think it might be a big one.

PART 2

AUTUMN

*I know it's not autumn just yet
but it feels like it should be ...*

Thursday, 7th September

My tongue doesn't want to taste it anymore

I am skinny at the moment; people keep saying it. Even my fingers are missing the flesh that holds onto their rings. I was riding my bike in Victoria Park, and as one of them started slipping over my knuckle, in the movement of focus I missed a few peddles on my bike. But instead of slowing I started moving, faster and faster, until I was out the gates of the park, and I realised that the wind had been pushing me along the entire time. I wonder how long I was flying before I realised that I was. It feels nice to be carried once in a while.

I am sat now looking out of the window of the pub, on the roundabout in the village. It is too cold to sit outside these days. I think autumn is forming in the air. I am drinking a glass of dark red wine, which is unusual for me, but I have been guzzling so much Sauvignon recently that my tongue doesn't want to taste it anymore, much like a few other things I tend to guzzle. These days are a little slower than they were in the deep heat of the summertime; I suppose that's because I want to be carried mostly, and I'm heavy from my heart. So I'm rolling like the rolling waves, and rollers being rolled into strands of antique hair. I've left the tidal for the people who like to fall through the water and right down to the sea floor. I used to like the cracks that came with descending fast and hard and fiercely. Cracks make one creative and more likely to try and fill them, but cracks also tend to make you feel like you might fall apart at any moment; that you don't have the energy to hold yourself together. I suppose it's getting colder now and I'm still not able to eat my dinners at dinner-time, so I would think I have other things I ought to conserve my energy for.

You in me and me in you

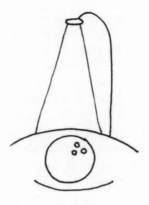

The sky is full of liners and a yellow, yellow toenail Moon. The street lamps are making the paths in the park glow an amber-orange sunset shade, making the paving stones look warm and peachy, whilst everybody's fingers are fingering the coins and keys and telephones inside their cotton pockets. I have been thinking of you today. Thinking of you, arms interlinked with a fair-weathered lady, in green and pink polka spots. She is peaking from under her hood, underneath the red-yellow end of summer sky. She is looking in your eyes to see if she can see me in you.

She will at first see you in every colour of the rainbow, whilst you take her on the love train in the park and buy her Pimm's, dotted with grape halves and other such exotic fruits. You will laugh awkwardly, and she will too as she tries to link her fingers in yours on the walk back from the carnival. At the end of the evening she will wonder at the way you said goodbye, whilst you watch her walk away, down moonlit cobbled streets and in September sunsets, bemused by why her hands felt like hot potatoes too soon out of the oven. Do you still see me in the cactus on your shelf or the Saint Christopher hanging by your heart to keep you safe on aeroplanes? Can she see me in the scratches on your back and the way that you fight back when you are wrong? I wonder, though, can she tell your eyes have always been blazing, like the hellish shine from a black spinning bowling ball, to make it so that when she comes as close, perhaps she only sees herself in their dark reflections, just like I suppose that I did. Can she see me in your penguin bedsheets, can she see me in the way you never call her when you should, on the telephone that you smashed, when you turned to hating me one Sunday afternoon in New York City? Weeks will form to months and she will wake up and wash you off her in the shower, the morning after you never showed and she was left wondering what might be wrong, or if what was wrong was loving you.

She will look into your muddy irises, and she will shout, 'WHY ARE YOU ALWAYS THERE AND NOT HERE?', and as she stares maybe she will see me in you and you in me. But as the days go on and you just keep rolling, I suppose it must have been only those sunny reflections in opium eyes that made me think I was so much inside of you. So much as you were inside of me.

Hair of the dog

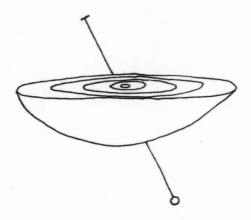

I am sick again, and I am sick of being sick. I feel like I see more of my toilet bowl than bowls filled with yummy things to make the heart stop hurting. In fact, the longer time goes on, the more parts of me seem to be quite unwell, and I wonder when dusty blue days turn into grassy green, pasta yellow, and primrose pink mornings. Yes, I do apologise for the blueness in my tone, it surely cannot last much longer than the sundown. I've come to get my bike from Victoria Park, and I am sat in a café opposite where I parked the other day, looking in at Thursday's ghost from over the roundabout. Over there is where I made a list of all the things I would do, whilst sipping wine, and thinking thoughts of gods, and September sunshine, whilst surfing in the blue lagoon, but today all I have done so far is twiddle thumbs and start to cry on my chaise-longue, before stopping myself in revelations that crying is for little girls, not big ones. It is too often that I dip my toes in the wishing well and fall right in, in need of being saved. In need of being saved often from the ones who pushed me. Why do we search for the cure in the very things that plague us?

Sunday, 10th September

Shine out from your insides

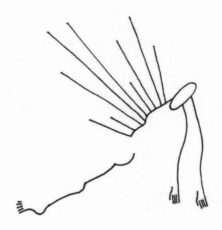

I have been missing you in-between heartbeats. It is hard to comprehend seeing as not seeing you is always what I've wanted, for myself and us. I know this is quite loathsome to say out loud, but although I do not want you here, some foreign bloodstream in me does, even just to talk about the weather or make me ravioli out of a tin for tea. It is strange when you lose a lover, even if your decision is to hate them, for their presence is missed in more ways than one. Your presence is missed in friendship and talking matters over picking TV channels, then lying beside you in bed for minutes too long, and moments too deep, to quite recollect the same again. When you stop to

43

pay attention, sometimes you start to realise you're losing the feeling, in the reminiscent moments, of blueness and yellowness.

Somewhere in-between dosing and waking up, I remembered about you, and all the things you liked to do on a Sunday evening after we ate roast dinners by the park. I am sorry that I made you feel as if I didn't care that we wouldn't stare at the clouds together anymore. I suppose I have only just calmed my red side, and realised just how wonderful we could be when we were pink and orange, and you came home from the plane and bought me an ice lolly from the newsagents on the street corner. I might have rushed to let you go but I needed to do so in order to find that pink part of me again that sung lullabies and painted my nails at the dinner table. I hope you're back to feeling pumpkin orange. You always looked the best when you lost your pulpy bits, and made patterns with the light that shone out from your insides.

Monday, 11th September

Princes and Prince Charmings

It seems the early evening has called for puffa coat-wearing, and hot chocolate on the side of Broadway Market. The earth is muddy down these ends; it doesn't feel much like the rest of the world. I speculate that the newer ones who live in the fields of London have all been turned two-dimensional, when they had their faces pressed on the pages of magazines, which I expect makes you feel a little different from the rest of the people walking poodles in the park.

People are walking mostly in most wonderful pairs. I imagine them with baked beans dripping off their perfect haircuts. I wonder, would they like each other just as much with the involvement of bean juice. I also wonder what it must be like to meet a body just like you, somebody that you agree with mostly so you do not argue about who washes up after dinner, because one of you knows that it's their go.

A man with braided hair dressed in pretty clothes has come to talk to me, about the journal I seem to be writing. He tells me he writes journals too and perhaps we should exchange thoughts on each other's thinkings. I should have asked him about his dish-washing courtesy. His name was Prince. I don't think he was one but he did have very glittery eyes.

I, a little more than he

I met a boy that seems to have a way of making me tell him all of my secrets. We drank wine in De Beauvoir, but perhaps I, a little more than he. He asked me about playing musical instruments and what I like for tea whilst letting silver smoke rings fall through his lips and into the night-time. At closing, the ladies in the pub fluttered their eyelashes at him as they told us we must leave, even though we didn't want to part, so he rode me home on the back of his bicycle in the pouring rain, and we talked about the world under the shelter the strange people upstairs made, by the water side, at my house. He has pretty eyes that say they want to kiss me, but they are not to be trusted.

I have spent a lot of my day thinking of him, and wondering if feelings can be real, if only felt by one. Does he always kiss people on the lips, like he did with me when I hopped off his bike, with the rain on our faces? I had always wanted to kiss in the rain, and it's only now writing this that I have realised I had done so by accident. I wish I knew it was coming so I could have taken it in a little more. Slowed it all down and saw the world happening. Maybe if I knew it was coming I would have told him not to. With that look in my eyes that I give my mother, saying 'stay away', when really I want her to hug me tighter than usual. It's not unusual for me to find fantasies to live in with strangers, thinking they might mend my heart. I did it for the last two years and I suppose I have only just realised that after all. I shall be doing/trying to do what everybody keeps saying to me I should – slowing down a little, maybe to the pace of the slugs in my kitchen ... so that maybe I would notice all those moments I seem to miss, like rain kissing, smoky kissing and last words exchanged over candles. Or when I sat on top of his jeans, and he hugged into my neck, and we laughed at how crazy we both seemed, living in my living room. I'm not sure if we will meet again. Half of me likes how mad I looked when I saw my eyes in his eyes, but half of me feels so totally, inexcusably out of control and scared quite, for my life and my tear ducts.

Preoccupations

I'm sat in my bed, which I don't usually do, except for sleeping times, which I'm usually laying down for, so I guess I don't really ever sit in my bed. This is a one off. My computer machine is whizzing on my lap and I can smell the remnants of a half-eaten Thai red curry in the bowl Olive left at my house. My tonsils are sickly and my focus is off, so I have eaten apples and spent most of my day thinking about running off into the sunset. Why is it that I am always there and not here? I am finding it rather hard to be still, inside these present moments. Mostly I do dreaming in bubbles above my head or make worried faces from thoughts of something I did last week. Both of these things are usually something to do with running in the sunrise, in consequence of all the running in those sunsets. Maybe I should have a fast from love. No more love, lust, or bits in-between. I will accept love, but only love, for things like omelettes and fairy lights, and long silky gowns. Maybe tomorrow I will go on a walk and find another new thing to add to my love list, and add one every day until there isn't any room left for thoughts of beings with promiscuous hands. I think this is what Tuesday's human has done for he seems preoccupied, maybe with things like almonds, the clarinet, and not saying goodbye: things which I don't really want to be preoccupied with myself, so perhaps we can't be preoccupied together.

Great big shiny beautiful stuff

GREAT BIG SHINY BEAUTIFUL STUFF——.

I am half-sitting half-lying on my chaise-longue. I have realised not all things beautiful are as appealing after you get to know them. Sometimes you just want to fall into an old blue friend with faded arms that can cuddle you the best. Beautiful things are good to look at but not to sit on or to hold for extended periods of time. Maybe this is the same with people.

Other times, the most beautiful people can be good to stare at on the underground, a safe enough distance away, but not to walk around with hand in hand. It strikes me that when you are next to something that looks so golden, you're only copper in comparison. I imagine my flowery armchair feels a little shabby next to my chaise because I found her perching on the side of the A23. She is still quite as beautiful though, even if she isn't as sown together. In fact, she might be even more beautiful because she's a little enigmatic and filled mostly with stories. I wish I could remember this when I'm standing next to the beautiful ones, instead of despising them for their skeleton skin, which turns everybody into pieces of melty butter.

The most beautiful types of people are the ones who are beautiful yet they do not know it. The ones whose laughter makes you sparkle; the ones who look good with a hangover and smile at you when they sense that you're slipping. Sometimes you catch these people and you fall in love and hate them all at the same time. You look at them through emerald eyes, and notice how they might just be a bit more better than you, inside their souls and in their sentiment.

Sometimes I think the thing that makes them so beautiful is that they are shining on the inside and it comes out through the pores of their skin, like glimmery gold dust. When you hug them or when they tell you a joke, it is disturbed on their surface; it settles on top of you, and for a moment you feel like you are made of gold stuff too. This is the sort of person I think that I would like to be. Someone once told me I was one of these people, however, these types of people rarely know they are one of them. So I guess you can never really tell whether you are them or not them, and that's of course what makes them beautiful in the first place. If they did know, then they would be back to not knowing because then they wouldn't be as beautiful.

Tinker

I have rushed in through the side entrance at the pub and before me stand five people. Three of whom I have shared a bed and two of which are girlfriends of two of those people. I look to the left, where the sister of one of the three is waving at me over a pint of cider and to the right where a familiar beanie-wearing boy I met at the weekend over schnapps in Frankfurt is leaning over a girl and patting her on the head. In anybody else's book this would be pure burning hot hell, but, well, see me, I don't think there's anything better than some drama over wine.

I start with the ginger pair; they are the easiest to handle. I am also well acquainted with his sister; it seems their sisters always like me more than they do, which does make me wonder, but it appears I do not have much time for wondering today. I say my 'hi's' and 'how do you do's?' I'm sure soon they will wed. I think my invitation will come in the post, but I'm still not sure she knows me and him used to .... you know what. So that all tastes a little like vanilla ice cream. In fact so does the single one, between my teeth, who has been calling me Laura since he arrived, through a popcorn-flavoured cloud from his electro cig, which leaves me slightly dazed and wondering (again) what made me kiss so many frogs. We do hugging and I float out of that haze towards another kind of haze, expected only, after ordering three large glasses of something really big, one straight after the other, another and again, for the last pair won't go down well through such low levels of sobriety.

So as I finally push my body from the bar, to get a sense of my inebriation and of whom else I might need to hide from, I find myself being engulfed by an embrace, or is it just a platonic type of hug you give a 'who', who is your friend and you are meeting with on the weekend for some breakfast sort of foods and chitter-chats? Well, yes, I think I surely am sensing my inebriations, and your heartbeat next to mine again and, without looking, I can tell which 'who' it is who is giving me such a mad taste of all the years I've missed inside their big square shoulders. And then it happens: the sword eyes. I can feel them coming from the side, straight into my irises. Actually I would say they are more like shots, from shotguns;

they are quick, and gone before I can catch them. I turn to find their beholder. There she is sitting with long twisty hair, all the way down to her knees, delicately sipping a yellow beer. I must say I did not expect this; I thought she would be more of a vodka soda, but yellow seems to suit her nonetheless ... and instantly I know that we have to be friends.

This is where my memory fails me, thank goodness, and all I can remember from then on is telling the boy from Frankfurt that he has oh such lovely ears. I wake up to find a picture of myself posing sexily in a pink toilet cubicle that had 'Eat shit' scribbled on the wall behind, and a message from my ex-lover saying 'You are a tinker' well yes Sam I am, didn't you already know that?

Thursday, 28th September

Pickled like pickly onions

I'm in bed before eleven, the world is chaos and I'm as pickly as the most pickled of onions. Whenever I think me and drama are friends, I remember she is the kind of devious friend whom tells all of your secrets when you aren't listening. Whenever I think I have her under control and right where I want her, she reminds me that I am a human, which usually means I have utterly no control over anything except what colour pants I put on, although there is evidence to suggest I might not be choosing even colours. Talking of pants: my belly is resting on the top of mine, it's full of bamboo and aubergine and fizzy, fizzy cola. Sometimes I like eating all of the aubergine in my Thai curry just because I know Reuben hated aubergine. I find tiny rebellions like these every day hoping they will stop my bigger ones but no such luck. I am in dispute with the sky. I am in dispute with the ground stuck to my sandals. I am in dispute with the water in the taps. I am in dispute with myself, with the paper I write on, with my mother when I force her to reason my reasons, to dispute my disputes. I am even disputing with my delivery man; he has been hiding my new brown rug.

Sometimes when you have marvellous storms, you have to find your sense of marvel, and in turn let the world marvel at you whilst you stand very still and let the weight of England's people hit you all at once with their weathers. There is a certain noise when the rain, the sun and the snow-storms occupy the same sky, and in the midst of ferocious feelings you think you just might scream to see if you can still hear yourself blowing in the winds above. Instead of roaring, I fall slow to concrete and let my head rest on the warm feeling of hard unconsciousness. Suppose I'm a bug squished on the floor. I wait for all of those people to stop shouting for a second, wondering whether to stop or carry on stomping. I will lie here low, until the storms have passed and the people have put their rain sticks back in their closets.

Sunday, 1st October

The smells of life

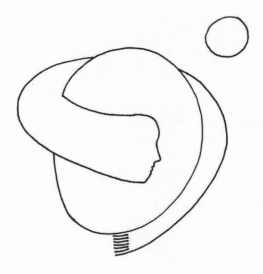

The landscape is grey and so are the people falling asleep on objects in the airport. People are in halves because of the night-time. I see torsos walking up to the toilet queue and legs at the vending machine. It is my third airport of the day and I have been awake for more hours than I am used to. I might be more of a quarter human; I think there is just my feet left to keep me moving forwards to Italy. Despite my snoozy eyes and lonely shoes, today feels like there are roses stuck up your nostrils, so no matter the shit, everything smells like romance and perfume.

I have been travelling an awful lot; I guess they told me that one day I would. So I have been watching the earth whizz past out of the aeroplane window so I don't miss too much, for when I'm ready to come home. I am feeling shiny still from the Burberry castle, and glittered from pink jelly and scones. They put me in tartans and gave me lots of sparkling English wine. I came away feeling slightly more sparkly than the wine and a little more criss-crossed, but more cross with someone whom which failed to attend due to forgetfulness and alcohol consumption the prior evening. Why am I so terribly forgetful and why are they so terribly drunk? I left feeling free though; I think I bashed out my last emotions on Augustine Valentine. I did apologise for my aggressive strumming, but she said 'that's what friends are for'.

11:04pm

Moon tales

I flew past the Moon in the night, before it got stormy and we jiggled about in our metal flying machine. I was reading of Mr. Dorian Gray when I looked up and there she was, hanging in the sky outside my egg-shaped window. Whenever I look I see the Moon. Sometimes I am looking for her, sometimes I am not, but no matter, she is there reminding me of magic and things beyond my understanding. I wonder ... how in so many little and big parts of sky can I see the Moon wherever I turn? Perhaps I just do not notice not seeing the Moon the other times, or perhaps the Moon is just for me. I prefer the latter, even though it is selfish of me, but sometimes being selfish in secret is ok. It feels good when the Moon watches me. It only means, though, that when I am stuck indoors or can't see the sky because the buildings are filling it above me, I feel lonely without her. It is like the feeling of lost love and wondering if it was better before you knew of such a thing.

She is my favourite when she is full. Mother Goose says when she is full she does strange things and makes people sad, happy or wild, which I don't think can make much sense when all of these emotions seem opposing. How can she make one person cry and another guffaw under the Moon-rays? She says that is the magic of her though, and with magic you never really know; that's why it is magic. I hope Luna isn't too lonely in the sky on her own. When she stares at me all mad and moonly, I hope she has comfort in knowing I am staring back at her, huge and humanly, 'cause sometimes when you are lonely, but not lonely on your own, you're not really lonely at all.

Monday, 2nd October

Lean a little

My shoulders are trying to sleep, and my liver is wheezing, as I am standing at the arrivals gate in Gatwick. So as my eyes search faces in the airport for somebody to take me home, I am already conscious of all sorts of deprivations making their way from the insides of my wibbly jelly-belly and out onto the edges of my skin, like wanting hands. Fingers caress the little blonde hairs sprouting out from inside of me, and nails stretch the flesh tight against my rainbow veins, so we are more see-through. We start to reach for things to make us feel full-up. I meet eyes with a stranger who stands with his feet apart, pointing outwards, just like me, and for a moment our stare asks: Are we waiting for each other?

I have walked and had my eyes open a lot this weekend. My eyes like my new boots and how they make us shine in the night-time but my toes keep butting in when we have been having polite conversations with air stewards, saying that they are not so fond.

I am in the car now with the taxi man; he is leaning into the steering wheel whilst letting snortels escape through the gaps around his singular front tooth. As we chase the other cars down the motorway, passing the flashing cats eyes, I get to thinking ... he seems like the type of human thing which doesn't have his skin pulled against his blood lines, and if he did you might see mayo in his veins from eating chicken sandwiches for breakfast, lunch and dinner, and maybe that might be quite lovely, you know. He passes me a yellow locket from its yellow crunchy wrapper, I think because we have been talking and I have prawn breath, but maybe he is just kind. The stars are sitting in the night-time outside my window, without the Moon – maybe she is hiding behind the trees – but perhaps now I realise the realisation that in my meetings with the Moon, wherever I turn, she is not sitting for me at all. I hope she is just sleeping, even though I know that she sleeps in the daytimes.

Oh I see her ... I just had to make a little lean, but that's ok, everybody has to lean a little sometimes.

Tuesday, 3rd October

Not so nice to meet you

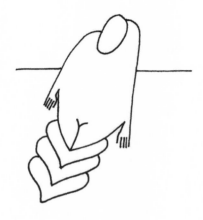

In life I have learnt that you can often see things a
mile off. You may spend time swirling and twirling
with your information, going from between and in-
between as to whether what is right is wrong or the
other way around, but what I have come to know
is this: usually you can see things from the hills
and the mountains and anything which is much
far, and high away. This is most true with the sorts
of people that come in on strings, rattling behind
more familiar people, like tin cans dragged in on the
backs of car bumpers, to make a big tangly mess,
sounding unnecessarily loud noises, weaving in and
out of relations and heartbeats. It seems there are

times you may be present in a life without your presence being known. You may be the thought in think bubbles and the eyes one sees when lying in bed underneath the night Moon. You might just be the face of a trip to the mellow, yellow seaside or another's misfortunate meander on a mundane Monday afternoon. Suppose you could be the soles of feet, standing on a gem-covered pedestal, or the face of a feared foe or ex(cellent) lover. So as I walk around the streets of London and think of you, a being I do not know, nor probably ever will, in turn I think of all the different beings which I know much too much about, for their nonexistence in my mortal hours, on this planet Earth.

I think of how you sit, with your legs twisted around one another, and smile in that saturated way that tries too much. I think of you skipping down corridors with blonde hair that has been left too long before you go back to the hairdresser, so all the golden bits look like they're trying to grow right out of your head, I suppose so they don't have to be so close to you, and perhaps because you're more of a muddy brown sort of creature. I saw you coming from a mile away, when I was having a picnic on Mars with Percival. I guess I didn't care so much then, because I was hot and fiery orange but now that I'm in Haggerston and the earth has begun to be blue beneath my toenails, I have come to think of it, and you, and I'm not so sure you are so good, or rather good enough, to be one of those little aliens that start existing in my brain, and have a name, and a way to say hello. Without any way of measuring the realness in the things I think about you and the thinks I think, when thoughts come to mind, about London fields and hot pink lipstick. I wish you would leave me so. Leave me to my afternoons of thinkings about watermelons, and other sorts of mysteriously large things. I imagine you aren't so large – certainly not larger than life, like an Atlantic pumpkin. You do seem quite large, though, when you're stuck to the insides of my head, like a papier-mâché balloon that cannot pop now that it's turned into something quite solid, all-consuming, and fat.

Sometimes you can say more with not saying anything

Last night I ended up on Olive's rooftop with La Luna hanging just by my head, behind, eating cheesy puffs. She doesn't usually add much to our conversations but sometimes you can say more with not saying anything; at least that's what she told me. I've been trying out this silent way of being. I'm near invisible, like feelings in the air between two lovers. Then I am gone all of a sudden in the wind, as sometimes does with love and other intangible things. It has been making people fume like cigarettes, but I hear they can be quite addictive, and every time you try to stop you want them that little bit more. So I suppose leaving is how you get people to stick around.

Peppermint

I have lots of men in different colours on my doorstep, offering me different kinds of sweets. The first is smooth and cool like peppermint. Another is sweet and then a little too sour for my cheeks. One is wrapped in riddles and very large words; sometimes he sends me books in the post. The last is just plain trouble-tasting.

I contemplate all these persons, and wonder which tickles the taste-buds on top of my tongue the most. I am mostly inclined to cocoa-swizzled chocolatey chocolate things, but all this dark milky indulgence has made me fat with anger, and fat like a plum pudding. Therefore, I'm trying things you can pop on your tongue in slightly smaller doses. I try to imagine the essence of them being chewed up and coming apart in my mouth, when I linger a little too long on one I almost wish that I didn't but know that I do. And I start to wonder: if I chewed mint leaves right before I slept, would I taste as minty fresh as him in the mornings? You see, the way that he wiggles and slides is in a bit more of a peppery way than me, as if he were a pepper snake, and the way that he talks and stalks around on his longer-than-most legs ought to be awkward but reminds me more of the cool reputation of a cucumber.

That night I laid upon my bed with his torso breathing the heavy scents of peppermint beside me, so fast and sleeping. I looked upwards at the faintly glowing star spots somebody once stuck to my ceiling and I wondered to myself if he really did exist. How could it be that one is so fortunately good looking and lively? I do not usually like the cooler temperament, nor them me. They try to cool me down but I'm too hot, like hot spicy BBQ ribs, and their ice cubes never melt – they only make me feel mighty scorching, as if I were a little fire in a red knit jumper. This little long mint seems all too tempting, not to cause a tempest with though, see. I wonder if we could cool and heat each other up until we were just like the temperature of the perfect bath. Perhaps this is the maddest notion, but I am full of them mostly, and mostly I am mad.

Monday, 9th October

Mon chéri, I am in love

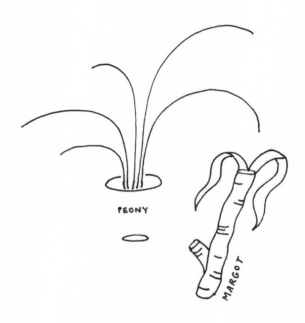

PEONY

MARGOT

I am sitting in my floral armchair next to Margot and Peony, who are sprawling out their green fingers across the corners of my living room. I am making lamb in cranberry sauce for dinner and I have been drinking cups of coffee out of blue mugs all day in front of my whizz pop. Life is lending itself a pinkish sort of orange sunrise in my eyes and everybody looks like they are growing flowers out the tops of their heads. Also, my belly feels a bit like glitter jelly. This weekend was filled with madness and lots of dancing on tippy-toes; so much so that today my mind hurts a little from all the fun and folly. I am trying to be calm, and considered, but really I want to run and scream that, mon chéri, I am in love. I am in love with love and life and dancing in the moonlight at the back of the garden.

You, you or you

I cannot read, or take tea. I cannot converse, for all thoughts make up of you, and my talking comes out in the sounds of the letters that spell your name. I want to scream that you are next to me, in all the bubbles floating around my head, but I fear we are too soon to take turns reminiscing recent weekends aloud to our friends and planning future flower picking, at two-step ceremonies in a chalet. I dance around the sounds and sit with a silence on my lips, which only says it more, just like the Moon does. In the reflection of my silent pupils, so bravely wide-eyed and wondering, you can see a pink spot glaring which, since I was three, has always told my mother when I am telling lies or trying not to tell anything at all.

I will wake tomorrow with the thoughts of finding other things to love again (I remember now, this was my original plan), so as not to get so inexcusably, sickeningly sweet, for all of my folly to taste like butterscotch. I am afraid they much prefer the darker tones in my hair, but all there is, is blonde: bleach fucking sunshine blonde – the whole thing a bomb of dazzling gold dust, glowing with an ambivalent but also so, so sure lust and love and roses and daffodils, smoky cigarettes out of your bedroom window, twisted up with green crunchy apples and tiny books for human hands about all the different types of springtime flowers. I hasten to mention that I am a mess and I am derailing from the rails which I built to stay on track, to keep me going in most appropriate directions, and I hate it more than onions which make you cry when you are cutting.

If only when I looked at you I were to exclaim something of intelligence, rather than to giggle and say that I am having fish fingers for supper. Where did the sureness in my sureness go? Where is the zig-zag-zing at the ends of my sentences, which queues the laughter from people's throats? More so, why do you put up with my talking of such inadequate things, which build to a mountain in my mouth, about a molehill that I found on wanderings through De Beauvoir Square? Is it my red cherry valentine lips and legs wrapped around your thighs which make my snortelling so very bearable, if not even turn you on? Turn you on to new ways of thinking about tea-times and cake-times and bed-times and times to turn the kettle on. I must think quickly of something much better to say whilst I am wrapped so inadvertently around your spinal cord, yet all I can think of is a silent and beautiful nothing. Just living and breathing and living and breathing in and breathing out, shake it all and settle on your chest, where your skin sits on top of your heartbeat to keep it inside of you.

Ribs rising.

Oh, what have you done?

Ribs fall.

I see your bones through your belly. You know you really ought to eat more jam doughnuts.

And with a sigh it seems …

I write about you, or I write about nothing. What shall it be mon chéri?

Perspectives & sticking together

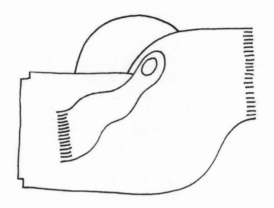

I have been battling demons all morning and memories all night. It seems my dreams are haunting me in the most infuriating way, which provokes tears falling out my eyes in the night-time. Earlier, I was having my morning shower to wash off the sadness in my sleeping eyes and where my usual dialogue would go a little like this instead it went a little like that, and that's how we left it: me and me, talking under the water, wondering why the happy raindrops from the showerhead weren't tickling the edges of a smile this morning. It doesn't make as much sense, as yesterday I got a bunch of purple daisies and a round of applause. I think it has something to do with my body walking too fast for me to keep up. So whilst me and my mind were trying to catch up with our outer shell (so we didn't get to feeling alone and all over the floor), we moved our feet too fast on slippery surfaces and fell right down that grassy bank of life you often stand right on the edge of.

So I lay there sprawled like a starfish in the dirt and I look up at the looming sky which, with a different perspective, has made me see that there are very heavy rainclouds overhead, coming our way, and we ought not go walking in the rain or we'll get sick to our skin and become sick to death and spend the rest of our days stuck to hospital beds. I close my eyes to think for a second too long and when they arise from being thoughtful, I see my outer shell hovering above, between me and the weather. Thank goodness she's come back for me. I guess from where she's standing she can't see the sky so well, and all she can seem to say is, 'why are you full of mud and sludgy things; so thick, and brown?' So we both extend our arms, in aid of helping, unsure of whether to go upwards or whether to go downwards. In a state of disarray, we stay frozen, in opposite statures, stuck in the air, stuck in the mud and stuck a little bit in the middle of life. The sky releases her rainclouds on us, and so the ground begins to cry, and so do the trees and ourselves, until there is water all around and we are sodden and sad, and we are quite under the weather and in the weather's hands. If only we could have been walking hand in hand when we began our morning stroll, and moved together with more consideration for the other and for the time it takes to have tea, eat lunch, pick raspberries from the garden, mow the lawn, earn enough money to buy a sofa – one I could have kept forever and start loving, and keep loving, and stop loving, and watch enough TV so that your brains fall out of your eye sockets when you're crying in the shower, but you tell yourself it's just the shower crying on you instead. If only we could stick together. If only we could have stuck together.

Short infatuations & longer ones too

I left Pepper's house this morning about 10am, after finding that he had placed an apple beside my head on the pillow whilst I was sleeping. I often catch him doing perfect things, and then questioning my own imperfect existence. I fear it only makes me fall deeper into the wishing well, but is he the kind of man whom runs away with you, and then without you? I will sleep beside him again tonight, in his bed full of pink ladies, and whilst I await his call I have been thinking: I do hate so that I have let this all submerge me quite so quickly, anybody else might have drowned. But I'm still under the sea looking at the fish, so I guess that I don't need to breathe anymore.

Sunday, 15th October

To things being things

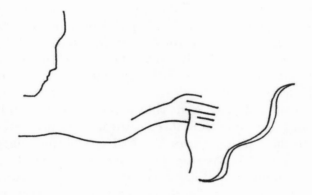

Wine and Olive go very well together on a Saturday night at The Shacklewell Arms. It all began when I was attempting to escape the inside folly of my mind, so instead I met with the folly of Olive's and a carafe of white wine. Many hours passed of hop, skipping and jumping. We kept it together for as long as we could, but faced with the smoothness of the smoothest sort of peppermint people in a late night bar, things seemed as though they might get rather odd. They talked of jewellery and us of mermen and then them of dictionary things, whilst we mused over made up words we thought might one day make us famous. Amongst mismatching of intellects, I thought that the real odds were whether I could keep this up. So we both giggled in the corner and wondered how crazy little things we might seem to less fuzzy sorts. I'm not sure why, but we clinked our glasses and sung out 'Cheers to making things things'. Olive went off dancing, but said to me she's always going to come back; just like a boomerang, she did, but I kept throwing her to the dance floor, as I knew that's really where she wanted to be, and not with me and the men speaking in twisty tongues, letting rolled up paper cigarettes dangle from their fingers as if they were things they wouldn't mind losing, like long-time lovers grown so uninteresting with their antique years. Whilst I was slurping under neon and they were sipping in the moonlit garden, I tried to get a look inside the insides of their pupils, to find out what the difference was in-between me and them. Whilst we looked quite the same on the outside, we surely weren't on the in, and how was I ever going to be on the in if I couldn't get in on the secret.

Monday, 16th October

The day the world went orange

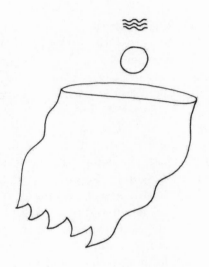

The world is orange. I have never seen satsuma weather before, but it is oh quite so beautiful. I stare up; the sky to the left is filled with sludgy brown. I wonder if lakes of mud will fall and make us all seem swampy. I stand in the doorway at Canalside and look outwards, whilst the insides of my house have fallen into the night-time, yet it's only 3 o'clock. Everything is upside-down, I am curious, so I ask the man in the den, who I don't usually talk with, whether it is just me who can see the tangerine world by the water.

The wind is blowing the bushes apart outside like he's mad as the devil with them. People are leaning off their balconies, across the water from me, with uncertain looks on their faces. I see their thought bubbles wondering whether to jump or to go back inside and finish their sandwiches. I'm not sure what is happening, but it is rather audacious for a Monday afternoon. By the time I have looked up from my pages we have gone full satsuma. I wonder if the world did end right now, would I mind as much now that I am orange, maybe I'll become an orange angel. As I muse ... the world ends around me. I think of all the things I'd like to do when it does become the end, but it's come too quick. I do not have the chance to be as great. So I sip my coffee on the doorstep and let my hair blow up in the wind, as if the aliens were trying to pull my plaits up into their spaceship, so I could come up for some tea.

I think it might be nice if the world was always different colours. Monday would be yellow because yellow is the happiest colour and reminds us of things like buttercups, pasta shells, sunshine, and cheddar cheese. Everybody needs a bit of something yellow on a Monday. Tuesday should be orange like today, for reasons I am unsure of, but sometimes you don't always have to have a reason, and sometimes you are unsure, so. Hump day will be blue like the ocean and the seas, and we will have tides inside us that make the Moon change. Thursday – the colour of pink roses, for the lusty valentines that can't wait for Friday, to sit and kiss under apple trees. At midnight everybody's fuchsia pillowcases will turn into red tomatoes and they will ooze crimson blood with yellow seeds, and Friday will begin. We will dine with the witches and all wave wands, and take to slurping on berry daiquiris whilst getting naked with each other in ballrooms. As the weekend comes around we will wake up with ice cold teacloths wrapped around our brains, and we will wonder what we were thinking when we were the colour of a strawberry.

THE CLOUD PEOPLE

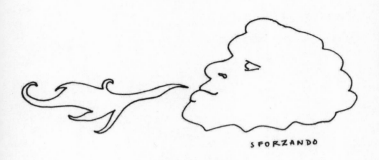

SFORZANDO

EUGENE

WOOZLE

Yours or yours

I am sitting at the Kings Head in a red velvet booth, which so perfectly matches my dress. I have holes in my sleeves, which lets the wind tickle my elbows when I'm waiting for the bus. I have spent the summer pretending, in more refined situations, that I had not yet noticed my frigid elbows. Rips and cavities taken into consideration, I'm surprised they let me through the big fat curtains by the door, that lead to such a fancy establishment.

There are exotics pinned against the maple wallpaper, and hung on metal rods that are straight, and much taller than I, and the people that marvel alongside me. The animals are pulling their most grisly faces, and I start wondering whether they died mid roar, or if not why the people thought they would want to look angry forever. I see one check his reflection in the mirror, and then suddenly we are all dancing the cha-cha.

I have been spending my days finishing my album, and it seems like it might be finished sooner than I thought. I ought to know not to speak too soon but it is fun to speak too soon, like when I speak too soon that I'm going to be getting lot's more apples placed on my pillows when I wake up in the mornings. Speaking too soon is just really dreaming a lot out loud and I love, love dreaming. The only dreams I do not like are the ones you can't wake up from. Last night in the middle of the midnight, I awoke in a certain madness, hanging off my mezzanine, searching for a someone, I realised I was alone as I guess I don't belong to anybody these days but myself. Belonging to only oneself is a dependable thing, much more so than being yours or yours, but in these times of gentle loneliness in the dawn, I wonder – is it better to belong but not truly, or endure a suffered silence when you sleep? And do we ever really know if we do or if we don't?

How do we know if we are meant to be where we are? I contemplate this on frequent measure, day in, day out, and day in-between. I think our belonging must change as frequently as we do, else my parents might still go to the beach together on Sundays. If something belongs forever, does it mean you haven't grown or changed or turned into anything new? Should we only start finding things to belong to once we want to stay the same forever? Maybe you can change at exactly the same time. Perhaps belonging together in the right way is like the red dress I am wearing. It is my oldest, but no matter how much I grow inside and out, it fits and looks just right. Perhaps it was too big to begin with, or maybe some things are for good and some other things are just for good moments and measures and fortunes and lead you to the longer stretches of perfection and well-fitting friends.

Wednesday, 19th October

If you were a fruit what fruit would you be?

London is amidst a foggy fog. I have been walking around art galleries all afternoon, arms linked between Valentine kisses, on cheeks, and foreheads. It seems Basquiat is something of a mad genius, and has conquered more by 27 than some could do in a lifetime. Perhaps the reason he didn't live as long is because he didn't have to. Maybe when you're great, time doesn't take as long. For me, time usually does, so maybe I am a dormant genius, like my chickenpox trying to erupt again. I do feel all the more inspired though, and I will make paintings for my wall with all the words Jean-Michel whispered to me in the gallery. I, too, want to be a Renaissance woman. I have been having visions underneath my mezzanine of creating a future masterpiece. I have been having visions of sun freckles and small socks at the seaside.

I have been having visions of you carrying tiny people on your hip, wearing sandals and eating miniature sandwiches ... How can it be? For I am not yet done with the world nor she with me. I do not have time for all of these co-ordinations and lurking in sunsets. I do not have time for night-dreaming, daydreaming, or vacant stares. I do not have time for anything less than solitude and attention. I find myself ambivalent and estranged from my lone self. I think I am becoming a pear. Are you becoming a pair too? And would you please measure your pearness and pear-shaped pairity, so I can put mine up next to yours and evaluate my sense of affections. Why do our minds think of things without us? Surely it is I who must command me to think, or maybe it's like telling your heart to beat or lungs to breathe. I am sure that is still me, though, only I do it so often I just do not notice anymore, like tying my laces and walking to the vegetable shop. These thoughts, though, have come from somewhere quite obscene. It surely cannot be me, you see. But if I ruled by myself, think, think, think, about late night dancing, and porcelain flowers, this might suggest I am ruled by her and not she by me. Why is she so disobedient? Wandering into green forests, and orange sunrises. Drowning in see-through waters and sinking in fresh snow beds. She really is going to get us both in a lot of trouble if she can't stay on the track. I will give her a talking to, but first I will finish today's dreams of you and I, for it does make the world a little sweeter for a minute or two.

Sunday, 22nd October

Armour

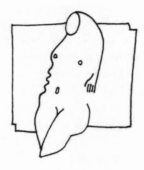

I am naked in a field watching movies play against the sky. The grass is tickling my thighs as the air makes it skit around beside me like little mice tails. The sun on my freckles feels all very congenial, somewhat like the way my soul feels from being so naked and free. As I laze, the wind comes from over the hills and caresses my body in his blustery hands. I begin to try and scratch him off, and as I do I become more aware of being so bare and so seen. I turn to find my clothes, but they are blowing in the clouds, up where the movies are playing; I suppose the wind has me naked now until he doesn't want to blow anymore.

I turn over and you are snoozling, next to where the small in my back was. My head is being like the thunder. I try to shake off all the frolicking. I have been drinking too many wines and tequilas with salt and limes, and not enough water before bedtimes. I have been eating way too many ham sandwiches and prawn jacket potatoes and Ripple chocolate bars and all things which make the belly squish, so that you can see me more through my clothes. I have been talking, a lot, about my feelings to friends, and sometimes strangers too, so that when I get home and sit at my kitchen table, and become all introspective, I feel exposed more so and without my outer. I am naked at the table. I am naked in the park, eating croissants. I am naked with my clothes on. I am naked at the movies. I am naked in your bedroom, looking for the duvet cover. I wonder in the mornings why you like being naked so much. Is it because you are contented or because you are fine with being seen, and do you like being naked at other times too? Your eyes open in a gentle, sleepy way and your teeth come out as you see me, seeing you. My eyes quickly escape under their lids and I turn to get out of your entanglement, but my limbs are stuck and my breasts are falling around inside the sheets. I am not sure I can carry on being so sure; I need my clothes back.

Little thinkings (a few things I've been thinking of a little lately)

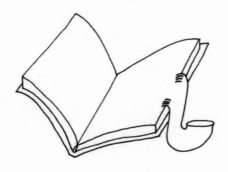

I haven't seen the Moon for a while. I guess that she is on holiday, much like my wispy soul. I have been drifting in and out of working moods, in moments, for weeks. Weekdays feel like a smear of something translucent and smudgy, whilst the weekends are full of late night/early morning sips from cocktail glasses and screaming on the night bus. In my vacation from doing anything worth doing I have begun drawing all of my plants with their names, so you know who I'm talking about when I'm drifting from friends to foliage but more so, so you can appreciate their haircuts. I may do this also for my guitars, or anything else

I name for that matter. I would draw pictures of the people in my journal, but I'm not so good at scribbling people, only writing them down. I might have to hide it from them anyway as they don't know they are inside a book yet and they might want to crawl off the pages.

It seems there are fireworks outside the window every night of the week. I have been chasing them in my slippers, trying to see the sparkly sky but I only ever seem to be able to hear them. Oh, they are such a tease. Berton is looking super spiky and green; he is almost as spiky as a cactus – I want to get him some more lime green friends, but I fear my brain does not have room for anyone else. I ought to save my brain space for my people friends, as every new name I try to remember I think I might be losing one I already know. In fact, I have forgotten the name of my small yucca and the boy I met at the bonfire on Saturday night, who dropped hot marshmallows on my shoes. All I know is that they both begin with 'Y' but I cannot think of any good 'Y' names. I must have been having a mad day. Suppose this really is true, I ought to make sure anybody new is much greener, and much, much, more mighty than the stalks that I already have wiggling and winding in my green house, else I might be left with all of the new and none of the things that fit when you're fat after Christmas.

My telephone has been boring. Nobody has called to say hello, so I am a little lonely, I suppose. Thank goodness for Berton, even though he's not so good at hugs. I have a pickle hangover, so it's making me unsure of my pickliness. A pickle hangover is the feeling you get from being a pickle thereafter. Sometimes I get it after the weekends, when I know I must have been a bit pickled and prickly. People don't usually mind me soaked in vinegar, but I can be a bit sharp for anybody new. You either love it, or hate it; it's just like marmite, only it's not, it's just like pickles, actually. What I mean is, today has meant much of nothing, except the aftermath of being soaked in vinegar and of being the shape and size of a baby cucumber. Let's hope tomorrow brings more colours and varieties of fruit and fireworks in the sky above my house, with the sound of big guns shooting down the leftover night clouds. I will look for the Moon tomorrow, in case she is missing or she has been wounded by the October festive sky activities and I am the only person who has realised that she is gone.

Tuesday, 24th October

The Moon, she is missing

Somebody at Canalside has stolen my orange bubble chair. My heart has gone raw, I am sure of it, and I have wibbly-wobbly jelly-belly from being on the bus. So today is not good. All of this misfortune started in the night, when instead of sleeping soundly I awoke with a startle at 1.43am with the sudden feeling that something was terribly wrong. I was unsure of what it was until now. The stars have shifted, you see, and I still haven't seen the Moon. The Moon, she is missing.

Ila's flees have been biting my ankles so I have scratchy feet, and my eyebrows are getting tired from being so angry, when they help me to look more closely at things and look fierce, like a stripy tiger. So up and down is all wrong. With all this taken into account I think we might have a very large-sized luna problem on our hands. Why does my pinkness feel more like bright gut-wrenching red? Where has the ceiling inside my head gone? Why is the sky so much darker so much earlier in the afternoons? I contemplate all of my questions, and realise I am suffocating in a turtle neck. Why do my jumpers feel like they are strangling the sense out of me? Well, that is probably because I have been wearing two at the same time. Maybe that is the key; maybe I have been doing things double. Loving, looking, thinking and scratching. Perhaps if I did everything in half-time the highs wouldn't seem so high and the lows not as low, and I could breathe again. But I've never been that good at half-measuring my affections, or other things.

Now the Moon, she is missing, and the sky is much darker like a giant sheet of marmite. The stars are crying outside, and inside there are noises in the night. Just like the ever-present stream of words forming doubts in my head, there are ghouls escaping from underneath the bathroom sink plug, trying to stay contained but ever so persistent, to haunt the house.

Appropriate swimwear

I am awake. It is 11.03pm. I have been in bed since 9.30pm, reading books and listening to the sounds at Canalside. I cannot sleep, for someone is crying next door, and I feel their sadness is filling the neighbouring houses. I have a bit of a sadness of my own to-night; I hope it is gone to-morrow with my cold. I hope it is gone away, with the sight of love letters in the morning.

Consistency is key to being happy, I do believe. How can one feel happy when you are happy, if your happiness is not consistent? Those moments of elation are surely brought back down with the promise of their falls. Well I suppose life isn't consistent in constitution. The only thing that ought never to change is my name and the colour of the sky, except for that day the world went orange, and except for if I become a pear on paper. Emotions though are ever-changing and ever-fluid, like the water in lakes. I like swimming in my lake. It is vast and when the sun shines you can see rainbows in its reflection, however when it pours the water hits the water in the most splendid yet interrupting way, as if the whole universe is disturbed, so that we must sit and stare and do only that. This happens a lot. It means that just before the storm, I have to stop and anticipate its ferocity. Should I get out of the water? Will it pass or will it be delightful to swim among the patterns made by a fiery heart on the surface top?

You never really can tell with watery things, and things that can slip through your fingers.

Right now I am on the side of Lake Laurel, eating cheddar sandwiches, with dirt stuck to the bottoms of my feet from the leftover wetness on my soles, which is sticking me and the floor together. I am watching and thinking and deciding whether I want to swim today, whilst the currents circle the circumference of me and draw the fish right into the centre, whilst they are taking evening showers. The lady next door lets out another shriek through the wall. I think she is being swallowed up in the middle, maybe her toes are tangled in purpley green tangle weed. I hope somebody will save her, because I can't find my swimming cap.

Wednesday, 25th October

October's secrets

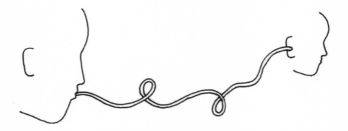

I am sitting in Mien Tay: my second favourite place for pho. It's very green in here. There is grass in the glass of the table, and the table is made from bamboo sticks. I am meeting Adé for phở. I have a new phở friend and that is one of the most marvellous things to have happened today. The lady across from me is telling all her secrets to the whole café but we don't really want to know. So I put my head down in my journal and think of all the secrets I'm still keeping from the people who might or might not want to know. I wish that I could write them down so their weight could be carried by the paper and not by my heart, but it seems as though the more people that try to carry them, the heavier they might seem. I wonder, is it more selfish to tell your secrets or keep them for only you? Sometimes I wish I hadn't known the darkness of my fellow humans. Is it better to know or not know? Because you sure can't unknow things and you sure can't uncry them.

Is a secret always best to only be a secret?

Saturday, 28th October

When my sister came to town

I was walking down to Leicester Square through Chinatown and I was talking to Anaïs about love. Anaïs told me, 'love is blind, that's why you loved Reuben', but I said love is not always blind when you're looking at the right sort of fruit. Love is all the more seeing because they look magnificent, especially in the colour red. My sister laughed and kept walking and exclaimed she couldn't possibly imagine me loving anything more than phở, and I said, 'yes, well I do really love, love phở', but what are the middle bits of love? The bits in-between liking and loving and falling, falling, falling, to your death or to your destiny. When his lips are like valentines and his eyes to me like the sun that shines into the edges of my soul, making me shiny and warmer ... What is this feeling, even though I know it is not love? So we kept walking and talking and linking arms and shoulders and hands, and sometimes legs when she tried to trip me over. We are one you see, we are one sister in each other and when it comes to love I couldn't love anybody more, so she seemed the right sort of sort to talk about with this sort of thing. So onwards we went on our adventure through the Big Smoke.

We tried on new faces at the beauty stores. You can't keep them, but it is quite fun to try on being fabulous. Then we had pink, pink fizzy Lola cocktails, with meringue and tequila and sherbet and sugar, sugar, sugar oh they were even sweeter than our faces. We ate sushi and then more sushi and crispy squid and noodles, and woodles, and lunch three times over, and saw our much fatter selves in the art, late night at the Tate, as metallic balls flew over our heads and sent us sleeping underneath on bean-bags. After all this fancy frolicking, we frolicked some more at The Shacklewell Arms underneath the Saturday night disco ball and in the Moonlit garden, with the smooth French ones that are always smelling minty. As my sister twirled inside a cloud of streamers with Pepper, I fell down a wishing well and all my two pence savings came in after me, from my spotty piggy bank, so I might just have to stay here for a while, until I'm spent. As the morning began we couldn't keep alive for any longer, so we skulked home with chicken kebabs in our palms and fell asleep on puffy pillows, amongst the other palms on my mezzanine. In bed that night I touched my toes on Anaïs' legs, and she said, 'I used to do this to you, do you remember?' and I said, 'Yes, you were smaller then'.

Sunday, 29th October

First one at the party

Last night was the night we would celebrate Halloween. I know it is on the 31st but we cannot be celebrating it on Tuesday! We have things to do in the week – we are quite important here in London! I started with slurping rice noodles next to a Zazzie pot, for some intelligence into her recent revelry and canoodling in the city. What we learnt was that everybody might as well stop trying to be so wholesome when they are in their twenties and rather be as bad as the devil whilst we can still get away with it. From then onwards, abiding by my newest set of rules, I proceeded to Adé's house for an aperitif, where things ought to get a little out of the ordinary. After knocking I stood back from the door and before me appeared a welcoming pair of hugging hands. Shortly after, I was ushered into an apartment where I was amongst a banana, a black kitten and a bloodied man. I stood for a while and, through awkward exchanges, it was decided I would have a drink. They moved towards the kitchen, and it was then that I noticed the cobwebs sprouting from the walls and pumpkin guts spewing on the floorboards. It occurred to me that Adé must take Halloween very seriously. The gang returned from the kitchen without my Pinot Noir, and before I could understand what was happening the kitten was kicking the banana's foot in a slightly aggressive way that pre-empted one to speak, and so the giant fruit pushed the sentence out of his yellow mouth, like a really lumpy bit of pie that he actually wanted to swallow, and so it fell right on the floor. I stood there with pastry and chicken gravy on my boots ... 'so who invited you?' Oh gosh, this is a little bit wrong; I realise I am the elephant in the living room. I am at somebody else's party and worse yet, I am the first one to arrive. Before I know it I am out of the door and straight through another one, next to a silver-skinned Adé. It occurred to me that this must be how it feels to take the wrong turning in life: missing the right road by only moments and finding yourself confronting a human-sized banana.

The rest of the evening was a tad blurry. I did dancing things and revealing secrets to strangers. I am trying to recall what else you do at a party but I think that's really it and probably why we need the force of alcohol to enjoy them. At some point in the evening I was faced with an ex-lover of a lover. This would surely be the first time that has happened to me. She had yellow hair and a square belly, and those eyes that I know because sometimes I do them too; they say, 'don't come too close, I still have a fire inside of me'. She was quite a bewilderment and I wonder if it was only to me that she was, as how could she have so many friends with such wild words and green, green eyes? Well I suppose love is a gentle thing, which isn't always dealt with in a gentle way but nothing came of female tempers and I was resting on my pillow tops by 7am dreaming of ghost-coloured clouds, and a thirsty type of longing. Until next year's drama over pumpkins.

Fantastic Mr Fantastic

How fantastic it is to feel so fantastic. I am at my new coffee spot, drinking what might be the most fantastic americano yet. My heart is full of puffiness and happiness and all the good-nesses, as opposed to the bad-nesses I often seem so fond of. All I can think of is how on earth to stay as fantastic as this, for anything else is surely hell, from these realms of the heavens. It occurred to me that I might just be in the right place at the right time, with the right people and the right length of pickliness. I might be having the right sorts of dinner on dinner plates, the right sorts of wine in my wine glasses. I also must be having the right sorts of showers, for I am glowing, knowing, and always feeling as delicate as the morning time. It is as if I am skiing down a mountain at the perfect pace of a professional. Have I become a professional at life and being luscious? Are my legs getting longer and my hair thicker and my brain more full of marvellous things? It sure feels like I am becoming and coming over the sunset hills, just like from inside of my dream-bubbles. I am not usually good at being contented but maybe this time I can ski a little longer, as perhaps the new me is better at lasting. Yes, maybe I can shake this rollercoaster way of being, and maybe I can sit just for a second or 1000 seconds. Maybe I can sit and watch the world from the bench on top of the mountain, before sliding down the snow and eating a large fantastic bit of life.

PART 3

SICK SEASONS & THE TOURING SEASONS

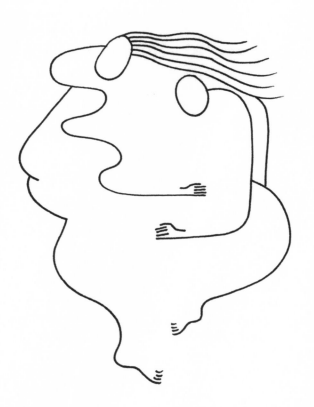

Tuesday, 31st October

Lovesick

I am sick. My tonsils fill my throat like oversized golf balls, blocking the way for yummy yellow things to go down and intelligence to come up. What's more is that they keep trying to talk with me, when we're sitting in the living room asking for pasta and bagels when they know we're only drinking spinach smoothies this week. I was sleeping last night, interlocked with Pepper. Our arms and legs and feet and fingers and hair and skin and lips and laughter were entangled and becoming a one. I woke up at 6am with my tonsils roaring at me and my head screaming back, 'Yes I know it feels a little like it hurts to fall in love'. It is now the touring seasons and the season I get sick, only I think this is a different kind of sick I've gotten this time. You see, though time is unsure in our calendars these days, I have never been surer of a thing like you and me. See, I have found the time in every single minute of today to think of you. I've got thinking you are quite good, even if you do make me sick in the stomach when I see you coming down the road. Yes, the only bad thing about you is that you are so good it makes my world seem worse without you in it. So even if they are only days, they will be the worst days of my life, without you by my side.

An extension of the beautiful ones

I am sitting on the train to Birmingham. My throat is making choking sounds and my bottom is vibrating on top of the leather train seat as the carriage pauses on the side of the platform. Today is the start of my month long tour; from here my entries could become dotted all over the world. I shall write, for you, my travel guide to touring. I am still unwell; my father has told me to be patient but he must not know me very well, as patience is a virtue I have never possessed. My sickliness has not stopped my giggling though. Today I had a full blown giggle, where absolutely everything is funny and the whole world shakes from one's chuckling. I think sometimes your laughs have been building up for so long that eventually they just have to come out, like tears do. I guess my giggles have been waiting for the very right moment to say hello again, and so here we are, making the train shake.

It is funny when you are pink like blossom and bright like a beaver with a bushy tail, how good things seem to happen. For example, the man on the coffee cart gave me a hot chocolate and I am going to put that down to first, him having a good breakfast and second, my giggling filling up the train with laughing gas. When I wrote previously about the beautiful people I think this is what I really meant. Their beauty is not in the shape of their nose but what they give off to the world in little energy pinballs. Little silver metal balls ping out onto nearby watchers and then ping back bouncing off their skin. The more they give, the more balls are bouncing and so their skin becomes polished and glimmery, and when you look at them they just shine like the sun.

The way to be this wonderful is to only let the sunshine through your skin, and not the raindrops, so you're all dry and don't have to let the collected rain out of your eye holes. I was thinking it may be exhausting to be this wonderful but really it is more exhausting not to be, walking around with heavy wellies and soggy tear-ducts. So as I was drinking my swirly hot chocolate on the train, I got to thinking; oh, how fun it is to be beautiful, and oh, how tasty it is too. I shall be taking an umbrella with me everywhere I go, just in case the rain comes again and tries to get inside my boots. I hope I stay shiny for good, now that I know, how much good fortune comes with smiling.

Wayward writings

My writing is becoming wayward; I put it down to all the fizzy cough syrup I have been consuming before breakfast time. Whenever I speak I come out in different sounds to me, and it seems I am always laughing. A certain folly has happened upon me and, instead of losing my cool, I think I am rather losing my mind, in an unrefined way that makes me snortle over popcorn in the car. How can one feel quite abstract, yet so put together at exactly the same time? I suppose I am a little like a splat of paint on a canvas. A splat that knows it was always meant to be a contemporary piece so didn't worry that it might not make sense to all. It is almost as if I have made peace with my madness.

I am in my touring season, but all I seem to see is the inside of a venue, so perhaps my tour guide to touring might not be as invigorating as anticipated. Life on the road is a shade darker than life with a built-in wardrobe. Jokes that are funny on tour would not be considered appropriate in the supermarket, and when you write them down in text messages they seem rather delicate ways of getting into serious trouble. I am back now for three days and, in an attempt to finally shift this angry bug that seems to have got stuck to my insides, I am going to stay in my pyjamas the entire time and flush him out with butternut squash soup and Lemsip, because I've heard he doesn't like those for tea.

It seems I am getting more used to more people being around a lot more. Most of my hours that were spent in contemplation alone under my mezzanine have been replaced with people dropping by for half cups of black coffee and orange quarters. I wonder if I will always like to live alone. Next weekend I shall be testing a life in Paris. Sipping espressos and hanging out of tall bay windows above people colliding on the streets below. I do wish I could speak French but it makes me all a little chittery and less chattery, especially when in the company of such smooth French fishies swimming the Paris ponds. It is enough of a task to speak even English eloquently with the ones who reside in the 'city of love'. I must eat only apples until I go so I am as slender as a French fry. It is more likely I shall arrive full of ravioli. Reuben has called to tell me he cannot eat anymore, for he is too sad. It makes me much too sad to think of him so sad, but sadder to curb his sadness with a dose of me for tea. I do not want to make anybody feel the blue tears, for I know how they feel too, but I think my efforts to make them go away might only make them come on stronger. Other people's pain tends to feel heavier than our own; sometimes Reuben tries to cure his pain with more pains, so he doesn't feel the first one so much. I have told him now though, as I have told him many times. I think he senses someone else in my tone of voice. Perhaps he will try to find a new girl with wavy hair and a wicked way of drinking Sauvignon. Perhaps he will find a new girl quite the opposite to me. I think that might be good. Maybe she will like watching 'Only Fools and Horses' and going to the greasy spoon on Broadway Market. Maybe she won't make music much too loud and say all the things she thinks far too often. I think she can make him forget to dream of love and actually make him feel it, and maybe he will love her when he's supposed to and not when he's not.

Wednesday, 8th November

Fizzy fireworks

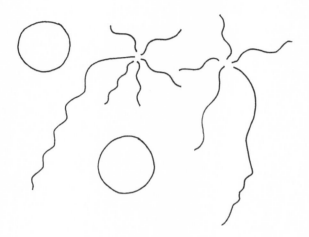

I cannot stop smiling all of the time. I look so cheesy, like a piece of Camembert. Grinning in the shower. Grinning through rides on the tube train. Grinning into my cupboard, whilst looking for tins of Green Giant. What a strange thing which I ask to be saved from.

Is it possible to be too happy?

Will my cheeks get sore from smiling?

I worry when I am this happy that it can only go downwards, as any more upwards and I wouldn't be able to reach the ground to walk around, but today I

118

shan't be thinking of that. I shall only be thinking of the happiness things, like playing sparkly shows with streamers and drinking glasses of Apérol under the watching eye of strangers, who know me all too well and not at all.

It is only one more day away until I will be striding in the 11th arrondissement, most probably sipping on cheap cocktails and chomping ham and cheese baguettes. I'm smiling now at cheese baguettes. Life is wonderful, you know? Maybe it can go upwards from here after all. Maybe I'll end up in the air, right above my house, singing love songs with the pigeons, but I suppose I ought to wear my hat and gloves, for it's beginning to be rather chilly in the clouds now, or so I've heard. Even though my insides are warmer than a pizza oven, sometimes when I'm this warm I burn from the inside out, like a fizzy firework, so that I'm tangerine and emerald and violet all over the indigo sky for everybody to squint at through their sunglasses. Unfortunately, I am about to pop and it might be a little too late to slow my paces and make this fire lasting. So I guess I ought to enjoy exploding and imploding and dancing next to the Moon in Hackney. And once I fall from the air into the river and I'm soggy and sodden and have to find all of my pieces again, I will remember what it feels like to rupture from being hot, like the fiery sun, and perhaps next time, I'll drink more ice in my lemonades and stay nearer to a fridge. I hope you are having a marvellous day. There are too few days in life for each of them not to be all marvellous.

Vive la France

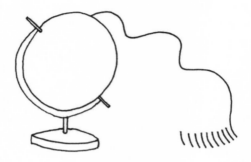

I'm moving in the direction of France. My eyes are wibbly-wobbly, my throat is like a raisin and my fingers are bleeding from being cut by knives in the kitchen sink. I am in a very tight pair of black jeans, because I was certain to fit into a 25, and as I seem to be going backwards my tummy is enlarging in them, from all the movement confusions. Last night I played love songs to sightly eyes, all dressed in winter clothes. It was rather swelling like my belly, and all my benevolent friends were there feeding me wine drinks and dancing me in hoops on their arms. Reuben sent his spies and they told me of how he is much sad these days. We reminisced of weekends in muddy tents and late night bars for a while, and before I left them I said: if we only realise we love things when they are gone, we can't possibly love them at all. The whole night was a façade of gold streamers and opinions. Oh, how people love their opinions and oh how they love to share them out loud. I wonder why we all have such a need to express ourselves. Is it because we are fizzy bottles of pop and when we get shaken we have to burst? If so, does that mean we can go flat too? Once you are flat like Reuben, how do you get your fizzy back?

I am on the train now, and because I have some time on my hands I have got to thinking: I have come a long way now that I have turned 23 and a half. I have come a long way since the me that didn't know where to go, or who to be. I was worried about becoming older, but I am starting to see its sunny side. With getting older in half years, the finest things have happened: I have lost all of my darkness, I have the longest hair I have ever had, and I have grown into all of my misbehaviours. I wonder where I shall be at 24. I wonder if I will be facing forwards: I do hope so as I'm feeling spiny like a globe on a spindle. I think I might like to live in Paris, and order croissants in a French sort of voice. I think I might like to wear longer dresses that get blown away with the wind and take me too, through to new horizons and cities with brighter lights and longer kisses. You know though I might like to be living exactly how I am right at this moment, because everything feels a little like something perfect. I am bubbling and I am brewing and I am on top of the skyscrapers in the city, smiling about all the fantastic things I have found in my latest half-year. Thank goodness I have finally started doing things in halves.

A Friday afternoon in Paris

I am quite tired because I have been living all night in my thinker. Now that my night stories are just my plans for tomorrow, does that mean I am living a dream? I have arrived in Paris, and I am trying out a French version of myself, writing my journals from a café terrace, just like I heard they do over here.

I have been trying to speak French to the French, but nobody thinks I'm very good, so I've returned to Anglais for my lunch break and ordered all of my food in my usual awkward accents.

I am trying to not write so much about Pepper, but it is hard when he is hanging off my hip bones, and twirling my hair in his fingertips. Later on I will be meeting his parents over bongo playing and Apérol. I wonder if they too will find my clumsiness charming, or whether my tea cup smashing hard down on its saucer will make their tummies turn and eyes ping from their place holders. I think I would like to be more graceful, like a duck that swims across the water without splashing. In life it has been said that I tend to cut some corners. I think I might be also cutting real-life corners when I walk through corridors and into the bathroom, because I always seem to be bashing my shoulders on door frames and always seem to be shouting 'ow!' Is it because I am cutting corners that I am clumsy in all these areas of being me? It comes to my attention that I again need to slow down. I want things fast and soon and in my face before I'm bored of them. I want to gobble my plate of pasta before it goes lukewarm. I want to kiss you quickly before my eyes ache, because people aren't as pretty in the winter. Short bursts of obsessions and infatuations for ramen and Mars bars and not brushing my hair so it curls in the wind. Short cups of coffee over minute-long lunches, throwing my scarf around my face and with a huff and a puff, blowing the whole place down. There's something fun about doing things fast, like the 100 metre sprint on the school field that is over before it's begun, and losing your mind in late night bars over tequila shots. Are some of us hot and heavy-footed and some of us cool and slow like a snail, with a burgundy shell in the late autumn? I wonder if that is why we appreciate each other in our different kinds, and also why we squabble over meeting times. Whatever it is I must slow down, and of course I must do it at once.

P.S. Eliot

I see you everywhere I look. I hear you in every word that is said to me, or seen in the streets on street signs. This thinking of you is quite impossible to maintain within a normal state of existence or exciting my senses for anything else but the affections of you. I try to distract myself with half-drunk coffees and polite conversations with freshly met men in cafés, but my heart has done that thing where it closes and opens only for one after tea times. Is it possible that you are quite perfect? Or is it much more possible that you are not, and that I am making a spectacle out of my attentions and thoughts leading always to you. 'Let us go now, you and I, when the evening is spread out, against the sky like a patient, etherized upon a table.' These infatuations dissected under light are much too strong to contend with. When you reach to hold my hands from across the table I cannot help but reach for them back and recognise my skin on top of yours. When I try to understand and depict the details of my love falling, I cannot seem to make them make any sense. For the few words we would exchange in conversation are instead met with deep set eyes and pulling of the hair. Will you lay under the sheets with me forever? Or will this fire in the fingers burn off in the night and leave us with an ash-filled bedroom, disturbing the air with a grey and murky mess of yesterday's thoughts and promises?

I divert my focus to the late afternoon, which is making the air grow darker around me. These hours alone feel most contented inside the city, and although you are not here, you surely are, as inside of my head you keep telling me off for speaking English to the people in the streets of Paris.

Saturday, 11th November

Giraffes can't dance

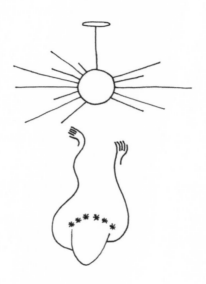

I stand in the middle of a mass of people, and where I thought I would feel at home, instead I feel an intruder in the dark. No one can see me dancing awkwardly under the disco ball, but still I can. In every shake of the foot and raising of the hands, I try to surrender to the underground showroom and join in with the people losing their heads under strobing light but, alas, I am a giraffe that cannot dance. I cannot seem to find my groove tonight; I think I lost it with the sunrise. I want to make a small escape, but I also want to stay because I know what it means to disappear. It seems to me as though my demons keep getting me when I'm standing in the sunshine.

It is my third day in Paris. I did not wake until noon, so I've only just eaten my breakfast and it's nearly become the evening. I am in the midst of the Bastille streets, awaiting a crème brûlée and an espresso, feeling more French, but still not as pepperminty. I shake a shiver at the thought of stunted conversation with elders and try to lose the feeling that something must be wrong in a moment of right. It appears to me that I am trying much too much and thinking much too much about my muchness. I recall, 'you're not same as you were before, you were much more muchier, you've lost your muchness' ... Have I lost my muchness?

I want to blow along with the breezy winds and land light on windows like wet raindrops. I want to be a laugher and a gentle chameleon. I want to evoke the devil in the eyes of strangers when I talk of moonlit adventures and scarlet tales of weekends in the countryside. I want to feel myself but not myself at the same time, this version is a little thin and dry. She does not make me proud to be her mother. She is the child that trips at the party and doesn't say thank you for her slice of birthday cake. She is the one that talks too loud in the restaurant or doesn't talk at all on first and last encounters. It is impossible to be one's best self in every single hour of our waking days, but on some special occasions I wish I could choose which self I had with my supper.

It is my last day in Paris before taking the choo to Luxembourg. I think of home and all the homely things, like beans on toast, and Berton, and a choice of people to meet on coffee breaks in the afternoon. I wonder if I like sitting alone in cafés after all, or whether I just made that up to make myself feel better about being lonely.

The rain is pattering and plopping on the street and yellow light from street side restaurants drifts out of windows and into the dusk. The city really is rather romantic and only made more so by French voices saying things incoherent to an English flower child. I haven't spent enough time trying the city on. I have played with it like a favourite friend that I've known for years and not asked it all the first-time questions you need to figure them out. I think I will be coming back soon; I like it here for creating and making impressions, and although I haven't figured the city out, I have started to figure myself out which, I would say, is quite a good trade. Thinking time and time to calm the nerves over a Pinot Noir, is the sure direction of getting back to being a Laurel. Perhaps I will find my groove tonight whilst I am dreaming.

Hong Kong hoola hooping

I'm high up in the air above the clouds and the Kookaburras, eating flaky croissants and sipping lukewarm coffee from a coffee cup. I have one hour left of my travel and it must be the first time in my life that I haven't wanted to get off an aeroplane. I am sitting in business class and I have my own little house, with a TV, and a bed and a bedside table and Vermicelli noodles for breakfast and midnight snacking mini burgers. I have a down duvet with a little pillow and rose water to spray on my face when I start feeling like maybe I might want to feel a bit refreshed, with seven cups of orange juice, a bottle of Moet, washed down with some red, white and pink wine, wine not? Is that what you're supposed to say to the kind man in the yellow outfit, when he's offering you a hot towel for your greedy palms. It is simply marvellous when you're flying so high alongside the sunrise and the affluent. I can see why the rich spend all their time getting richer. I am heading to Hong Kong to sing some songs and lay out by the sunshine pool. I have been informed that we have plans for immediate karaoke with a suntan. I have been giving a pep-talk to my tonsils as they keep complaining, but we are flying over the oceans in a metal flying machine and we ARE going to be on top of the world in leather pants. I suppose all this darting around is making me a little sick between the teeth but not so much to stop me dining and dashing around, like a sparkly star in the autumn. We are about to land so I must go; I shall keep you up to date with my movements and let you know just how sunny the sunshine swimming pool really is.

What goes around comes around

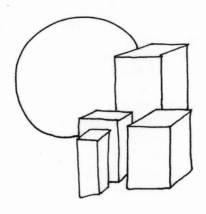

I am sitting in the sky next to all the Hong Kong sky-liners, drinking more OJ, and listening to the sounds of the swimming pool water sloshing and sploshing and splishing around on the roof. I am working on my suntan, so I can get back to being sunny and sensual through the winter times. Last night we danced in the neon town. I had my first tastes of karaoke, drunk on dirty margaritas and getting lost on the escalators, which cannot seem to decide which direction to go in for so long as it takes you to go the way you're going. I had so much fun that my laughter turned into a sickness in the night and I christened the million-dollar marble bathroom with a spicy sort of cocktail. You really cannot take me anywhere and especially not anywhere nice. Now I'm laid out on a sun lounger, three orange juices down, searching for that yellow ball of fire between mountain high blocks of concrete – turns out the sunshine swimming pool wasn't so set out for a sunning. My head is being a bit of a nuisance; I hope she will stop hurting before we have to play. Or perhaps we've played too much, I wonder, in respect of my bathroom tiles. I have been thinking that, yes, I guess what goes around really does come around. Me and the shade don't much want to be friends, so I'm off now to the Mongkok Market to find a piece of treasure for my Mother Goosey, to make her more happy. Life feels pretty good these days. All this flying around and landing in places almost doesn't give me time to think of anything sad. Life feels full of life and love and friends and really good sun hats.

Sunday, 19th November

Let me tell you the crazy thing about suitcases

Mother Goose said today, 'so let me tell you the crazy thing about suitcases', she never got to finish that sentence, as it was too good to quantify what would have only been a disappointing answer, as what fantastic end could have matched such a fantastic beginning? I wonder if this is true in so many cases of things which materialise quickly into genius and angelic form. How can things with such enamouring beginnings continue to enamour the senses for longer than the freshness that they hold, like a fizzy firework or a hot chocolate before it is a cold chocolate? It's just like that lust that distinguishes in the midnight before you wake up in the morning in the sore arms of a stranger. Are all things most fantastic never lasting? Or are the most fantastic things only ones with equally fantastic durations?

I'm sitting at Oslo on Amhurst Road, sipping a sour orange juice. I still have the leftover Hong Kong rain in my fringe and the snoozy way you seem to feel when you flirt with time zones, like a time-traveller. I ought to get back to my house and wash my roast dinner dishes and finish packing, but that thing that keeps me breathing has got me wondering in the streets if I can see you again, before seeing you again in a couple of weeks.

Tomorrow I go back on tour. I am going on the bus and they will give me a bunk where I can sleep all through the moony night, and miss home, in my new violet pyjamas. I hope the people on the tour bus will be friends with me, as I'm coming on my own, and although I like to be alone, I don't so much in groups of people. I cannot remember all of their names, so I will have to be sneaky about finding them out so they don't get upset when I can't remember the most important thing about them. I wonder what the most important thing about me is, is it that I am Laurel or is it that I am a Laurel and all things amounting to me make up the letters in my name, and when people say Laurel they don't just think of L.A.U.R.E.L., they think that I don't like tea, or bananas, that I sing on stages and find very complex ways of saying anything simple? Do names just become triggers of feelings towards personalities and does one Sam sound different from another Sam because they like eating different kinds of chocolate pudding? I sure think so, you know. Maybe that's why you can grow into your name. I wonder if you can grow out of them too.

Sad from shining (Vienna)

I cannot believe it is already this late. The year has passed me by like a cherry red train, chugging loud and very speedily towards something far away that it thinks it needs to get to quicker than I suppose it actually does. I'm sitting in a room much like a Coliseum, so that when you call out, your words come back to you like dogs with sticks. I am eating soup filled with pasta strands but it is about to be time for tea, or so I'm told. Everything is new. I am trying to learn, quickly, the rules of the road – when to talk and not to talk, what toilets you're allowed to do what in and how to drown out the noise of footsteps past your forehead, on the floor outside your bunk. I have decided to not spend any moments missing home but the lump on the roof of my mouth and in my throat hurts whenever I swallow, so that I pull this face that reminds me of the way that the sun looks at me when it's sad from shining all alone in the sky for too long. My mouth is making mini stretches to tell me that my insides feel like going to bed. I really should be more of a granite rockstar, or a sparkly emerald, but I'm too wayward to stay in one direction for two weeks and too weak to sing on stages full of sparkly stars, with a black marble sort of hangover.

Tuesday, 21st November

Poland and beyond (Krakow)

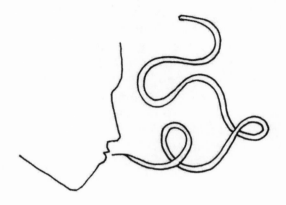

I am sitting in a red velvet room in Krakow. I have slurped half of my hot chocolate with a spoon made for miniature people and I am wondering why on earth they would make their spoons so small, as I haven't seen any elves around the town this morning. The skies are dark in the city; they have been since the morning. Not many people stop to say hello. Instead they keep their heads down in their laps, twiddling trinkets on market stalls. I have ventured into the square to make the most of my idle hours, in-between snoring on the tour bus and chirping on European stages. I have settled more into touring life, after eleven hours of bus sleep it turns out being next to the stairs is quite good for when you need the loo, and when you want to peer out of the window because you can't tell if you're going forwards, backwards, sideways, or up. I have bought Goosey a flower reef to match her blossomy way of being, and also one for me to hang by my bed for when I'm feeling snoozy and sick from not being at home. Maybe I can find home away from my house on the water, in my little black coffin bed, or maybe when the bus keeps moving in the night, deep into Poland and beyond and I am dreaming in my sleep about Percival and Pepper and Peony and Margot, I will get quite sick from moving so fast, so far away, so quickly, in the darkness.

Somewhat reminiscent of a rainbow (Warsaw)

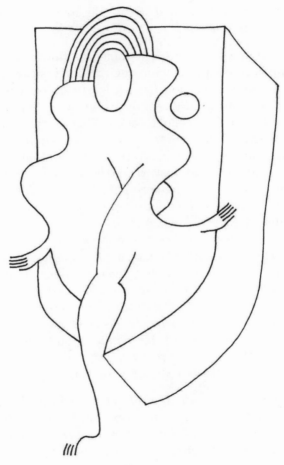

139

My head has been a little headstrong as of late; it's been stopping me doing silly things, telling my heart it knows better than she does, which, to be fair my head usually does. Most importantly though she has kept her beating, enough to make both of their feet walk forwards, in a straight and concise sort of way, for a while now.

I have always been accustomed to finding goals and impossible ways of achieving them. This can be good, especially when you have a lot to do on your to-do list, except for the speedy haste by which one must achieve such excellent tasks. This morning whilst I was making coffee stains on my fresh pressed bed linen at my hotel in Warsaw, a little think passed through me and disturbed the air for a second in the limbic system, where my feelings are at large. In this fleeting moment of quiet displeasure the heavens came down on me, and roared so, to suggest that I might acknowledge the oppression that had been brought on oneself, which was blistering through my chest like a cigarette burn coming out from the inside. My heart became a hole and my mind an open sore, spilling out brains and grey matter. My feet got twisted in my bed sheets and my hair got wet, like there was a big watery cloud hanging right over the top of my pillows, and for a moment I was stuck, in a state of dripping discontent.

When you become fixated on great big golden goals, sometimes the in-between becomes just that and all you can see is the end. I suppose I have been missing some emotions on the way there to my future, and now that I'm standing at my pearly destination they're catching up with me, like my cumbersome contenders in the race to heaven. With the weight of the oceans, they are on me, like the flies on the dead. I fall fat and heavy, straight through the clouds, 49,000 miles to home, just as I was turning my key in the lock. Sometimes when I'm falling and feeling all at once, I look around and see that it is rainbow weather, as if the sky can't make up his mind. Whilst all things are opposing around me, I spot a rainbow arching, full of joy, sadness, fear, disgust, pity, shame, love, envy and indignation. That's how I'm feeling today. I am unsure. I am not sure and I am surer than the surest sun. I am an abundance of colours arching in the sky over Poland whilst the sunshine shines and the rain rains, all over the people walking pathways in the park. My colours will say – the storms will end and so will the sun. What a thing to feel, even if those feelings are not what I feel like feeling today.

Tuesday, November 28th

Scwibble, wibble, brains on the floor (Copenhagen to Stockholm)

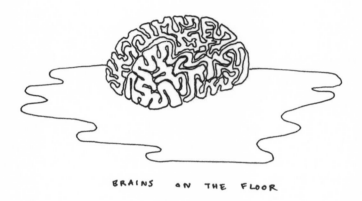

BRAINS ON THE FLOOR

I am writing to you from a winky-wonky table in Stockholm. I have just arrived, with a winky-wonky way of walking, talking and looking at myself in the mirror, because last night my wine glasses towered so high they made me topple from the sky, right onto the ground, next to my bunk bed. I took a few days off from the tour people to mix with some others that remind me more of home. We went riding on wild horses on the Copenhagen coast whilst the wind tried to take us away; I nearly let it but it felt so wintery on my cheek bones I had to go back. We skulked in graveyards under umbrellas with fists full of Merlot, trying to find Hans Christian Anderson under the ground, who once imagined Aerial under the sea, when the darker hours called upon the daytime. When I returned from my holiday hours everything appeared to be quite different than it had been. I was met with sour lemon melon faces and a white cupboard with yellow daisies to sit and wait in whilst the show went on. In an effort to make the best out of the not so best, I played a motherfucking rock show and then went to a smoky bar to talk of my transgressions and woes with friends. I will sit today with my thoughts that I have been trying to mop up but instead seem to be making more and more of a mess with, on the floor of my mind. I will be mainly wondering why I'm always being such a pickle monster, and if everybody is a pickle or if it is just me who makes such odd becomings of situations which ought to be ok but never really are when I'm involved.

Happy birthday to Mummy Goosey (Oslo)

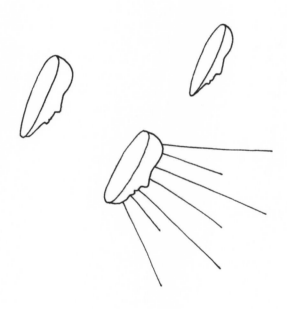

Today I feel like a buttercup, melty and yellow and spurting out of the green, green grass awaiting the honey bees. I could tell you whether you like butter, or you might already know, in which case I could tell you who I know doesn't like butter and that they've been making it rather hard to be oh so flower-like. So, feeling buttery, I am sitting at a table in a coffee shop, hiding from the city snow because it is hard to move when you're stiff from being in the fridge. It is 2pm, and already the sun is getting dark outside the doors. On the street people pass and momentarily take refuge inside the fluffy feeling of being next to a radiator. I am meeting with some other buttercups today and we're going to plant ourselves in the fresh laid snow, right next to the water at the edge of town. It is my Mother's birthday; I would like to make a small tribute to how fantastic she surely is and therefore everybody must know. She is fantastic in the wind, when her hair blows on the beach and she makes tiny grins. She is fantastic when the sun shines and turns her face more sunly and full of suntan. She is fantastic in the snow when the insides of her nose freeze up in Finland, and we fall on the floor laughing because she has crashed into a tree on her snowmobile, and she is most fantastic when it is raining and she makes everything seem as if it is not. One day I hope someone will say that I am as fantastic as my fantastic Mother.

Furry (Hamburg)

Today my writing begins with the needing to get
something out of me. It appears that there is a
big furry critter stuck to the edges of my insides.
Sometimes bits of her pink fur slip out of my pores
when I am not thinking straight, and instead of

paying attention to lessons and learnings, my mind goes wayward and all I can see is her pink furry skin, coming out the holes of mine. It was ok when she was smaller and I was too, she was still a little more little than me, and even when I opened my mouth too wide, in loud exclamations so that you could see her in the back of my throat, people didn't mind, as how was I supposed to know any better that she was there?

Now that I am 23 I don't really grow as much as I used to, except for the ends of my fingernails and the roots of my hair. However, monsters don't have the same rules as we humans do, and she has started growing out of my ears and eyeholes. Sometimes us two get into some terrible trouble, especially when we are wearing the colour red to dinner or we put on high, high heels, to make our legs look long, long, long. Sometimes we throw the dinner off our plates or say the wrong thing, much too late, after bedtime. When we are then alone lying face-down naked, atop a table covered in white towels at a spa, and the lady leaves to make some mixtures to keep the furry in, it is in that second too long that she is gone that we will start to fight. It is these times in solitude that I will realise that I am not in solitude at all, and when I'm thinking, I get to thinking these thoughts are only thoughts that a monster could think, before I thought them so. So I will say to myself, and of course she may hear too, 'I wish there was a potion to make your fur less vibrant, and manners less vulgar over red wine and confit duck'. Only it would seem my words, which make her hurt, only make her cry louder out of me and so we expel our bad tempers, like a tempest over Hamburg. The only sure way I know to contain my critter is to turn off our telephone and hide ourselves in French restaurants, from the people on the streets, pitter-pattering their footsteps like human raindrops plopping on the pavements of Germany.

It seems the more that she might grow, the more days we will be together, in-between the right and wrong and after some time you don't know your bottom from your belly button and you start to think you might just be all bad news. See, when there's something foreign inside of you that's been there for a while, it might just become as much of your soul as you are, and in an attempt to get it out or fight it off with poison and/or poisonous words, you might just end up killing yourself at exactly the same time and whilst you're slumped in a floral armchair dying, you will wonder: does that mean there can't be one without the other?

Maybe the only sure way to let her go is to let her go wild, hoping she'll grow tired by the time that it's time for tomorrow's tea, and we can spend the evening cleaning up all that we've knocked down in our tumultuous tempers. Maybe if she's let wild she won't feel as wild, as she must do in the depths of my belly full of pudding, high on sugars, and crimson jelly. For I suppose without the room to grow, how could she grow into the shade of all her hot pink furriness, and how can you learn from your misbehaviours, without being allowed to have any? Yes, I suppose I ought to let her feel the air on her hairy ears, and London concrete between her toes. I do fear we might not have any friends left after we've shown off all our pink sides, but perhaps they will have pink sides too, and perhaps they might be even furrier.

Neverlands (Nijmegen)

It is the last day on the tour before driving back to sunny Hackney, to open the doors to my riverside cabin and fall into green plant-like arms, made of all things terrific and tantalizing. It is funny how life passes, as if it hasn't yet begun. Passes with the weather and the seasons and lunches. It just does, like the rain does and the world does and the sky does; it's just one of those things. So, if no matter what time does happen, in the end, does it mean anything at all? I wonder, do all the things we do mean anything, or are they just moments gone in other moments? Like moments gone in dressing rooms in Nijmegen. Eating cheesy pizza, stocking up on free snacks from the fridge.

Shortly after today, tomorrow and the week after next, will I think of this again and recall it just the same?

Does it matter that it has happened if it doesn't make ripples down the shore of my mind for the rest of forever?

Is it worth it to endure skimpy seconds of smiling?

When I'm driving down the road towards home in the morning, am I driving to a place that is worth remembering or just another thing that is as unsure as every day on tour in foreign countries? If every second is as fleeting as the next, I ought to try and take them all in a little longer than I already do, but on my time away I can mostly say I've been thinking ahead: thinking of thoughts of bed by the water, eating only apples and trying to cool my temperatures so I don't kill Pepper with a golden fever; drinking only mango juice till I'm giggly and wiggly and overdone from spending too much time indoors with Augustine, Persephone, Earnest and Emory. I wonder if Berton has missed me just as much as I've missed his spiky way of saying hello in the morning. I wonder if Olive has missed us sharing our nothing minutes together over cake, and

I wonder: does Pepper miss all of me or miss me at all? I wonder is the water still green and the sky still tangerine in the evenings? I wonder if Ila has dyed her fur a different colour for the Christmas season, so she's become a Christmas cat. I wonder if the whole world can be different in a few weeks or will everything be just the same and like nothing ever happened.

Pint-sized portions

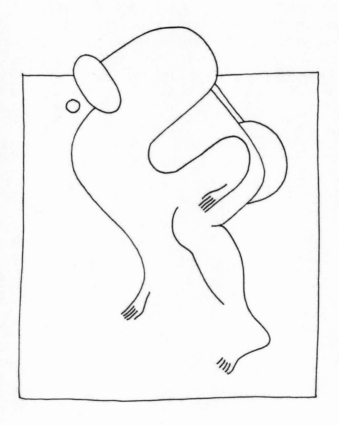

Since I've been away the sun has fallen out of the sky and the slugs have been locked inside my bathroom, having tea parties under the heat of the light bulb. Things seem different, even though they are not, like my belly is much more round-looking and wobbly, full from eating ham and cheese sandwiches every day and people don't call to ask me for my weekday plans, as they assume I'm still not here, even though I am. It is good though when you aren't always here, as when you are again people seem to like you better.

Drifting, as drifters do, but in the best sort of way

Everything is perfect like a pink puffy paprika. The whole world is glowing, like a neon glow-worm; from all the smiling we have been doing inside of my house on the side of the canal. As I get older things seem to make more sense, and in turn everybody else makes more sense around me. They all seem to be getting wiser, and I more similar to them or them to me, and we spend most of our time eating roast dinners and making standing ovations for the entrance of new friends who have come to dine with us.

I am here. I have arrived as a Laurel and all these mutterings I have been contemplating have been revealed to me, as just me and the only me I am or ever could want to inhabit. I am frightfully in love with the world and she must be with me, as I heard when you love someone you want to sprinkle happy dust on the palms of their hands and in the things they eat for breakfast, so when you see them you get to see them smiling – one of those smiles you only can get from someone else stretching your cheeks apart, and then you're both smiling because you made each other smile, and you realise you might be those beautiful ones on the side of the flower market, looking like the Australian summer. There is no happiness better than the happiness you get from giving all your happiness to somebody else.

Usually in times of absolute elation I worry of my deflate, when I've run out of fresh squeaky helium collected from all the birthday parties I have been invited to over the summer months, but I'm floating so steadily up in the clouds that I almost could be one of them. It doesn't feel quite like its usual whiplash on a rollercoaster, but something more of a mad drifting under moonshine. Up I drift and along ways I go, over the poodles at the market stalls, past the windows of the people reading books inside of yellow houses and right through the start of the cold weathers in November and straight towards the springtime dogviolets. Drifting really is the best sort of way to travel in the wind.

Drifting feels quite good on a Monday and a Tuesday and a Wednesday, Thursday, Friday, Saturday, Sunday afternoon, as long as you're drifting in the right sort of direction and, on occasion, even if you are just hovering above a spot of muddy terrain. Drifting feels quite good, like Pinot Noir makes you feel good; also like when you eat the softest chocolate-chip cookie with a gooey inside, and all the warm makes your heart melt and be nice to strangers. Drifting smells a lot like the smell of Spyke my Christmas tree, and looks a lot like Olive's mother's porcelain baubles, hanging off his spiky fingers. Drifting sounds a lot like Roux when he is laughing or Pepper when he is speaking his sub-morning voice, before he gets naked in the shower. Drifting tastes like strawberry sherbet for breakfast, but when you feel it underneath your toes, it seems more like the type of lambskin slippers you might get for Christmas. I am drifting, drifting, drifting, in and out of dreams, and realising life has become something I might see upon my eyelids when I am sleeping, or at the movies with my Mother Goose. If only this time last year, when I was writing letters to myself about being lost, inside my chest and tummy, I could have known about drifting and how wonderful we are when we stop running and screaming and looking in certain directions, with specified shopping lists for all the things we need to get when we go into town. If only I could have known to pause for a moment and take the biggest breath I ever could take, so that my body would puff up just like Violet Beauregarde's and I would be purple and floating over all the people that told me I couldn't fly. Well no, of course I can't fly you silly goose; humans can't fly! We can float though, in swimming pools and in the sea, on our backs, in stripy swimming costumes and even in lakes, on top of the tangle weed of our darkest emotions. As I lay in the shape of a star looking up at the sky, I can tell things really are all quite sublime, as instead of falling back asleep in the mornings, days have become better than dreaming at night, and all I want to do every single day is live, live, live, every tiny second that the gods will let me do so.

The end, or the start, whichever way you might want to think it be.

POEMS

Unrequited

Swear to me your undying, undignified love
Leave me dripping in the paints of war
never before would I have imagined you, in the
  clasps of my heart
leaning on the veins which lead my blood so
  devastatingly to you.
And which way would I turn which way ought
  I look?
you must be mistaken, I was walking this
  way anyway.
Now running, but not from you to you,
running into empty arms half closed,
shielding your body from the sheer mass of
  my madness.

I have been with out you far too long,
I can feel it in the iris of my eye, which sees
  you everywhere
I feel like crying more, more and more
as you never liked, like I thought before
Ruin me, in whichever way you please
I come to you a servant at my knees so feed me
fill me with life's food, and make me full.

I have lost my wholesome heart
before we have even started to grow
maybe in a year or so
maybe in a week
I will remember all the lessons I learnt in my
  adolescent years

in my youth, my younger youth, not my older now
I am twenty I am a woman I am I am I am
Green eggs and...
I am
Whatever I want, No
whatever you want me to be.
And what if it is my own that you wish so tenderly
The tenderless bruises of my soul, will never quite
　　recover from the rejections of you
The projections of unrequited, self-assured, and
　　high esteemed evaluations
string me upside in a butchers, and leave me
　　for parts
our hearts caged
only for ourselves to roam freely without them

Marry my soul, you did the first time I met you
Paint my minutes in years, and seemingly there is
　　no measure to the end.
I asked how I ever might I mend, you said you
　　didn't even know that I was broken?
It is my fault, I indulged you, divulged my sins to
　　the ever listening, ever discomfiting world around.
My senior, my soul provider of adrenaline, I cannot
　　sleep, I cannot eat, I cannot play the piano
No tea, no conversation to converse about
　　these problems
I am ill of you.

To live without you must surely be the only way.
To live in loss of love must be the only way to live
　　at all.

Am I expected to understand
or is it this way you wanted it so?
I suppose you are the only reason I wear sadness
    for clothes
bare me naked on the sea
it is a long old walk this life I have chosen, maybe
    I shall see you at the end.
And if this is the end and you are gone for good
    this time
I won't forget your name, should you ever
    forget mine.

Sea girls

I bide by the sea.
Close my eyes and touch the blue that meets
   the land
On painted shells and golden sands
To call the maidens 'I have come to join you!'
Replace my nails, with scales, and my skin, with
   a fin at the end of my feet
Give me a voice so beautiful no man shall resist
   my cry
Hear the heart song of the women that disguise
   their love for hate.
By the sea, the men lounge upon the beach
watch the water ladies. They feast
Eyes watered with despair for the women they
   once loved
Swim out there, in the great deep blue.
In the salt of a broken promise
or the break of a worthless glance.
Their faces empty silhouettes,
and their heads slightly balder.
He will wait there to find me.
With shells upon my breasts
Lonely at best, my organs soaked in salt.
Protect them from the harm in your charms.
I have come to mend and grow
Sea girls wreathed so beautiful.
With a hook wedged in my heart
however should I start
To heal?

Luna

I live in a portrait of my own
I sing in the mornings, and at night
and sometimes in the day, and in my sleep,
and while I shower, when I'm sad, and tears are
   all I have
inside my soul.

You called for me
You saw dreaming in my eyes
You all said I was the one.
The one that they would want
forever.
The one, you all would want.
the one who could be best.
I didn't need the best,
perhaps just a little better than the rest
maybe that's why I have always felt alone.
Just a little.

Stars hang around my shoulders.
sometimes they feel heavy
they tell me they are cold and sometimes I whisper
   to them
that I am sad.
Even when I am full floating in the clearest of
   the skies
the world can only see half of who I am.
and half of who I am supposed to be
The rest of the world has always looked so far away.

Craters plucked through my wholesome body,
    eat out my middle
But I am not to be eaten
I am not to be enjoyed
I am to be loved.
But not by everyone
Just by someone

Is it so wrong to crave the hearts of others?
Is it wrong to want the worship of their hands?
Sometimes I am crescent, just for them
I know they like it so.
I can see the reflection of myself in their eyes
as they glare at me through telescopic
    looking glasses
awaiting my every flinch
asking for my every breathing detail.

I, like some god who beckons sweet wishes from
    the sky
Strike lightning, whilst I stroke the thunderous
    lips of the far away planets
that hide in the corners of the universe
so far you could never reach them.
So far, that sometimes I am not sure they are
    even there.
Darker still they laugh in clouds of candy kisses
and make you smile, bigger grins of infamous joy
until you are a slither of cheese.
Since when was I made from anything but myself?
Was it you that did that to me?
Why did you tell them that?

You hold my back whilst I light streets strutting
  on shoes as tall as scrapers
So long as they are taller than yours I think.

I am frightful that when you - the sun, hides
  behind this heavy rainfall
I might not shine anymore
Without you I may be no more than a reflection
of dollar signs and bleach brave arrogance
beside the stars,
the people might not see me so well.
You ask me: do I want that?
I need you. That's what you say.

But you want me because I am free
You need me because I am more than you
I am something you can not understand
bewilder at my eyes
and wander around my feet asking
What happens inside my mind.

Without you I may be darker
I may feel heavy in the day
I may not shine out of the papers
and glisten like a pop preen princess of the galaxy
I may be further from this world
I may not stand brighter than any other in the
  darkness of the skies
But I will still be here
And I will be free.

Illustration & cover design by Elliott Arndt
This edition © 2019 Laurel Arnell-Cullen
First published in 2018 by Laurel Arnell-Cullen
Published by Faber Music Ltd in 2019
Bloomsbury House
74–77 Great Russell Street
London WC1B 3DA

Printed in England by Caligraving Ltd
All rights reserved

ISBN: 0-571-54110-0
EAN: 978-0-571-54110-2

To buy Faber Music publications or to find out about the
full range of titles available, please contact your local music
retailer or Faber Music sales enquiries:

Faber Music Limited
Burnt Mill
Elizabeth Way
Harlow CM20 2HX
Tel: +44 (0)1279 82 89 82
Fax: +44 (0)1279 82 89 83
sales@fabermusic.com
fabermusicstore.com